"I shouldn't have said I still wanted you," Katie said.

"Because it's not true?"

"Because it would be a mistake, and we're both old enough to learn from our mistakes."

"I'm the guy who plunged down a mountain with a bum knee and almost killed myself. Because I was too stubborn and impatient to wait for the all clear. I'm not known for being levelheaded when it comes to things I want."

"Like skiing?"

"Like you." He slid his hand behind her neck and pulled her close. When his lips touched hers, she leaned into him with pleasure and shock.

She had forgotten how good he tasted. A tiny hint of chocolate from the mini éclairs at the fancy salon lingered at the corner of his mouth. She kissed it away. Quin groaned and shuddered. It had always been like this whenever they touched. Raw insanity. Endless need.

"Quin..." She whispered his name, dizzy with wanting him.

* * *

After Hours Seduction by Janice Maynard is part of The Men of Stone River series.

D0451057

Dear Reader,

My husband and I have visited Maine several times over the years. We love the diversity from north to south, the fact that it is so different from our home in East Tennessee and, of course, all that magnificent coastline!

As I kick off this new trilogy, I'm giving you a hero who is being forced to make some major personal changes. In the midst of all that, he has to spend time with the woman who dumped him.

Poor Quinten. His life is a mess, and now it's getting worse. I hope you enjoy seeing Katie intersect his path...again...and watching how the two of them try very hard not to fall in love.

Happy spring and happy reading!

Janice Maynard

JANICE MAYNARD

AFTER HOURS SEDUCTION

If you purchased this book without a cover you should be aware that this book is stolen property. It was reported as "unsold and destroyed" to the publisher, and neither the author nor the publisher has received any payment for this "stripped book."

HARLEQUIN®
DESIRE™

Recycling programs
for this product may
not exist in your area.

ISBN-13: 978-1-335-20911-5

After Hours Seduction

Copyright © 2020 by Janice Maynard

All rights reserved. No part of this book may be used or reproduced in any manner whatsoever without written permission except in the case of brief quotations embodied in critical articles and reviews.

This is a work of fiction. Names, characters, places and incidents are either the product of the author's imagination or are used fictitiously. Any resemblance to actual persons, living or dead, businesses, companies, events or locales is entirely coincidental.

This edition published by arrangement with Harlequin Books S.A.

For questions and comments about the quality of this book, please contact us at CustomerService@Harlequin.com.

Harlequin Enterprises ULC
22 Adelaide St. West, 40th Floor
Toronto, Ontario M5H 4E3, Canada
www.Harlequin.com

Printed in U.S.A.

USA TODAY bestselling author **Janice Maynard** loved books and writing even as a child. After multiple rejections, she finally sold her first manuscript! Since then, she has written fifty-plus books and novellas. Janice lives in Tennessee with her husband, Charles. They love hiking, traveling and family time.

You can connect with Janice at janicemaynard.com, Twitter.com/janicemaynard, Facebook.com/janicemaynardreaderpage, Facebook.com/janices maynard and Instagram.com/therealjanicemaynard.

Books by Janice Maynard

Harlequin Desire

Southern Secrets

Blame It On Christmas
A Contract Seduction
Bombshell for the Black Sheep

Texas Cattleman's Club: Inheritance

Too Texan to Tame

The Men of Stone River

After Hours Seduction

Visit her Author Profile page at Harlequin.com, or janicemaynard.com, for more titles.

You can also find Janice Maynard on Facebook, along with other Harlequin Desire authors, at Facebook.com/harlequindesireauthors!

For Anastasia—

You were the first to make me a nana!
I love brainstorming book ideas with you... :)

One

Quinten Stone's older brothers had been aggravating him all his life, but this time they'd gone too far. Thanks to their meddling, his ex-lover was on her way to his isolated house. To live and work with him for a month or more. He didn't know how he was going to survive.

As an old man of twenty-eight, he bore the weighty title of Chief Operating Officer at the outdoor gear company the siblings owned jointly. That was enough responsibility. The last thing he needed to add to his agenda was juggling unresolved feelings for the woman who had dumped him.

Now his frustration had reached the boiling point.

"Butt out, you two. I'll make my own decisions."

Except that it was far too late.

Katie had already agreed to come. He'd be damned if he'd let her think her presence would affect him. That her defection had wounded him.

The three brothers sat in oversize armchairs in front of a massive stone fireplace. Had they been so inclined, they could have roasted a pig and had room to spare. But it was July in Maine, so the hearth was empty.

Farrell, the oldest of the Stone brothers—better known as the mad genius inventor when Quentin and Zachary were in the mood to tease him—leaned forward with a scowl on his face. "You've made some dumbass moves recently, Quin. According to the surgeon, you're in danger of injuring yourself permanently if you don't do what he says. You might never ski again if you don't give yourself time to heal."

Never ski again...

The knot in Quin's stomach clenched.

After his brothers, and their company, skiing was what he loved most in the world. And not so long ago he'd been one of the *best* in the world.

He stared at the angry red scar bisecting his knee. Eighteen months ago, in the car accident that had claimed their father's life, Quin's entire right leg had been mangled. He'd had three different surgeries, the latest of which was a complete knee replacement. Six weeks of grueling physical therapy had him back on his feet and walking fairly normally, but the surgeon insisted that ligaments and tendons needed time to recover.

Quinten wouldn't have been in such a mess now

if he'd been appropriately cautious after the first two surgeries. He'd been desperate to prove he was still the same man he'd been before the accident. So on New Year s Day, Quin had strapped on his skis and tackled a punishing hill in Vermont.

Unfortunately for him, his not-quite-rehabbed knee had given out. He went down hard, slamming into a small clump of trees on the edge of the run. Help was with him immediately, but the damage was done. This time, the leg was so jacked up, it couldn't be repaired. Hence the new piece of metal in his now-bionic knee. With every painful step, he was hell-bent on getting his life back.

He was desperate to ski well again, to carry his part of the family business, and to enjoy recreational sex with no messy emotions involved. Was that so much to ask?

When Quin said nothing, Zachary continued the gentle harangue. "The doc wants you to take it easy for six more weeks. With Katie here to help you work remotely, you can rest *and* keep up with your responsibilities. It's an ideal solution, Quin. Give it a chance."

The Stone brothers shared a landing strip, a small private jet and a kick-ass helicopter. None of them spent more than two or three days a week at head-quarters anyway. But it was the idea of having his wings clipped that made Quin feel like he was suffocating. Or maybe it was thinking about facing Katie that caused his chest to constrict…

"I don't like having strangers in my house," he muttered.

Farrell grinned. "You can hardly call Katie a stranger. We've all known her forever. I can do without my incredibly efficient admin for six weeks. Reluctantly."

Quin lurched to his feet and paced. The noose was growing tighter. He and Katie had been an under-the-radar item two years ago. Right up until the moment she dumped him with no good explanation.

Katie had been employed by Stone River Outdoors for six years, and Quin didn't feel comfortable pursuing her once she pulled the plug on their relationship. Not to mention that his pride had gotten in the way of asking for answers.

No one in his personal or business life had an inkling about the affair. Katie hadn't wanted gossip, and Quin agreed. Now he couldn't tell his brothers the truth. Katie was the *last* person he wanted under his roof. She'd made it clear they were over. Living together, alone in the Maine woods, would be incredibly awkward. They might have unresolved issues, but he had no doubt the chemistry was still there.

"What about *my* admin?" he asked. Quin had inherited the amiable employee after his father's death. The woman had been with the company since the first Bush was in office. She was set in her ways and flummoxed by new technology. But at least she was *not* Katie.

Farrell winced. "First of all, she's kind of a train wreck. We can either fire Mrs. B outright or find her something less taxing. Maybe give her a nice retirement offer. Katie will help you find a replacement."

Quin sucked in a sharp breath at the thought of Katie helping him with anything. He clenched his jaw. "What did Katie say when you asked her to come here?" He and Katie had managed to avoid each other for the most part since their breakup. But she *did* come to his father's funeral.

Despite everything, Quin had been oddly comforted by her presence.

Zachary stood as well and stretched. "She told Farrell and me she would do anything necessary to keep Stone River Outdoors up and running. A hell of a nice woman. It's asking a lot to put up with your sorry hide.'

"So true." Farrell glanced at his watch. "I've gotta run. Meeting a contractor in twenty minutes."

The brothers had suspected for some time now that they were the victims of corporate espionage. Two of Farrell's designs had been scooped and rushed to market. The new products were inferior and not exactly what he had been working on, but they were close enough to raise red flags.

To handle the disturbing possibility, Farrell had decided to make some changes. He hoped to work exclusively at his vacation home here on the northern Maine coast during the coming months and not at his lab in the Portland headquarters. Hence the contractor.

Quin felt the raw taste of panic. "I can work remotely on my own. I don't need any help. Nor do I need a babysitter. I swear I'll take it easy."

His brothers stood shoulder to shoulder, their sympathetic expressions like acid poured on his screwed-up life. Farrell jingled his keys. "We know you, buddy. You push and push and push as if the sheer force of your will can do the healing. But it doesn't work that may. Maybe in endurance training, but not in this. Six weeks isn't long, Quin. And we're not deserting you. We'll be around more than you think. It's not a prison sentence."

Zachary sighed. "It sucks, Quin. All of it. Losing Dad. The accident. You being sidelined with medical crap. I get it. You're on the edge. I can tell. But follow the doctor's orders, and you'll be a new man."

Katie had boxed herself into a corner when she gave Farrell and Zachary her word. Farrell was her boss. Zachary signed her checks.

Though both men had emphasized multiple times that her participation in this unorthodox experiment was entirely voluntary, she couldn't in good conscience say no. Stone River Outdoors needed her.

Quinten needed her.

Her anxiety rose, even on a lush summer day with the sunshine beaming down from a brilliant blue sky.

At Ellsworth, just before the crowded tourist playground that included Acadia National Park, she turned onto a less traveled road for the last leg to Stone River. Here, nobody but locals traversed the winding rural highway. Nothing much to see but acres of forests and fields and peaceful ponds and lakes.

The looming confrontation with Quinten tightened her stomach and made her palms sweat as she clenched the steering wheel. Two years ago, he'd been her lover. Even now, the truth of that statement baffled her.

Quinten Stone, by any definition, was a wealthy, larger-than-life athlete and playboy. After missing a gold medal by half a second when he was a teenager, he had continued to compete on the world stage. Both Quinten *and* his brothers were accustomed to traveling the globe.

Despite the fiery attraction she and Quin had shared, their lives—and their values—had been too different. Katie thought money was for helping people. Quin had spent his fortune recklessly, including the many outrageous ways he'd tried to impress her.

Katie didn't care about trips and gifts, nice though they were. She had yearned for a deep, intimate relationship. But Quin was one of the most emotionally closed-off men she had ever met. A sad cliché, but true.

When her GPS lost a signal, she was forced to concentrate on the road rather than Quin.

At last, she found the turnoff. Katie had never been this far up in Maine, but she had seen aerial photographs. Three spectacular homes sat on rocky promontories overlooking the sea. Almost two centuries before, a Stone ancestor had acquired an enormous tract of pristine wilderness and had named the small river meandering through his property after himself. Subsequent generations sold off the bulk of the land, but the current Stone brothers still owned several hundred square miles. They liked their privacy.

She had been warned about the gate and was armed with an access code. The paved road must have been wildly expensive but necessary. In addition to Range Rovers, Jeeps and ATVs, the brothers each had various automotive passions that wouldn't take kindly to harsh treatment.

Quinten's indulgence of choice was a sin-black Ferrari. Sexy as hell. Once, during her short-lived relationship with him, he had taken her out on the open road in the sleek high-performance vehicle—at midnight. They'd been far from Portland on an obscure two-lane highway that was relatively straight. When Quin unleashed the beast beneath the hood of the car, the rush of speed had been exhilarating.

Even now, Katie could remember the sting of wind on her cheeks and the tug in her chest every time Quin accelerated. He'd been in his element, laughing and teasing her when she gasped and squealed.

Later, he had found a secluded lane and made love to her on the still-warm hood of the car.

Katie sucked in a breath and felt her breasts tighten. Everything about Quinten Stone had been perfect for her—as long as she ignored the zeros at the end of his bank balance and his inability to connect with a woman emotionally.

Slamming the door on those painful memories would not be easy. Actually, it might be impossible.

All around her, the forest created a lush, green tunnel. Ash and aspen, spruce and pine. Beech and butternut, juniper and fir. No wonder the Stone brothers came up here at every opportunity. Unfortunately, all roads came to an end, whether the traveler was prepared or not.

Katie parked her Honda Civic at the base of the steps and stared up at the house. Quinten's house.

It was magnificent. Made of cedar and stone, it nestled among a grove of evergreens. Enormous plate glass windows were meant to frame the wild expanse of ocean and horizon. Today the sea was placid.

No one came out to greet her, although she suspected the aging Toyota sedan parked ahead of her belonged to an employee of some sort. Slowly, she climbed the stairs. She was ridiculously nervous.

Almost twenty-four months had passed since she broke up with Quinten. In the interim, she had made sure to know when he was in the building at headquarters, so she could avoid any awkward encounters. Though her office adjoined Farrell's, it was easy enough to duck out when she knew Quinten was likely to visit. That only happened when both men were in the Portland office at the same time.

Eighteen months ago—at the funeral for Mr. Stone Sr.—*of course* she had spoken to her former lover. Quinten had been tense and strained, still bandaged and on crutches in the midst of his grief. Her heart had broken for him. They exchanged a few words, and then Katie had moved away down the receiving line.

Knowing how close Quinten had come to death had shaken her badly.

Now here she was, more than a year later, about to step into the lion's den. She shook her head, though no one was there to see her dithering. The lion's den wasn't really a suitable metaphor for what she was feeling. People were scared of lions. Worried about being eaten alive.

When it came to Quinten and Katie, she *wanted* to see him. The scary part of the situation was her own abysmal lack of control.

Quinten Stone was the only man whose touch she had ever craved. Even knowing he was all wrong for her, it had taken every ounce of determination she possessed to break off the relationship.

Now she was about to undo all her brave, good work. Every sensible decision reduced to dust.

She tiptoed toward the nearest window and peeked inside. The place looked deserted, though she knew the impression was false. The master of the house was in residence. That was why she had been summoned to work here instead of Portland.

Unfortunately, she had left her sunglasses in the car. She closed her eyes and squinted skyward, warming her face. That was a mistake. Behind her lids, images of Quin danced dizzyingly. Smiling. Laughing. He was six foot two to her five-eight. At one time, he'd told her he was glad she was tall, because it made *standing-up* sex easier. And then he had proceeded to demonstrate.

Oh Lordy. Her head ached. A band of tension

wrapped her skull. What was she going to say when she saw him? His raven's-wing black hair and deep blue eyes were as familiar to her as her own.

Once more, she turned and looked through the glass. The furnishings inside intrigued her, though her line of sight was partially hampered by heavy, masculine drapes in navy and burgundy. Those thick window coverings were necessary insulation in the dead of winter.

Her pulse fluttered. She wasn't going to faint… Was she? She was scared and rattled and desperately anxious to see him. Pressing a hand to her stomach, she took one last look before she rang the bell.

As she lifted a finger to touch the buzzer, a sound at her back made her spin around. She tripped over her own feet and landed on her butt.

The tall, lanky man staring down at her managed a lopsided grin. "Are you casing the joint for a robbery?"

"Of course not," she muttered, her face flaming. "Hello, Quinten."

His brief nod acknowledged her greeting. "Katie…" He grimaced. "I would help you up, but I'm still working on keeping *myself* upright."

She scrambled to her feet, desperately glad she hadn't worn a skirt. "How are you doing?"

He shrugged, his expression guarded. "Depends on who you ask. I'm damned tired of people worrying about my health."

Two

"Maybe you should quit feeling sorry for yourself and be glad you're not dead or paralyzed."

Quinten winced. Possibly *this* was the other reason his brothers had sicced Katie on him. She didn't suffer fools gladly, and she didn't tolerate whiners and slackers. She ran Farrell's department like a tight ship. Because she was both impeccably fair and incredibly compassionate, her coworkers loved and feared her in equal measure.

It dawned on him that he couldn't actually offer to carry her suitcase. Well, he could *offer*, but the outcome wouldn't be pretty.

Had his silence been as long as it seemed? Seeing her like this after so very long had him tongue-tied like a middle school boy. His heart pounded and his legs were weak, even more than they had been recently. "I didn't think you would agree to come here," he said bluntly, wondering if the memories of what they had once shared tempted her at all.

He sure as hell was tempted.

She wore her sunshiny blond hair up in a ponytail today, but he remembered far too well what it felt like to have that pale silk waterfall stream across his chest.

Big brown eyes surveyed him warily. "I didn't think you'd allow it," she said quietly. "So I guess we were both surprised."

He took a deep breath. "Maybe we should start over. Thanks for coming, Katie. I really appreciate it. So do Farrell and Zachary."

"You're welcome. Happy to do it," she said, shielding her eyes with one hand and staring out at the ocean. The surface glittered like a million diamonds flung beneath the sun. "Your home is lovely, Quin."

"Thank you." The stilted conversation was polite, but it covered a thousand unspoken memories. Katie wore a pink silk button-up top with the sleeves rolled to her elbows. Slim black pants hugged her legs. Simple silver sandals exposed feminine toenails painted shell pink. Was it bad that he wanted to nibble those toes? He cleared his throat. "Let's go inside."

"Of course." Katie was clearly nervous as they paused in the expansive foyer, though she was trying to hide it.

He gazed at her intently, trying to mask his frustration at not being able to bound up the stairs. "I've been bunking down here since the surgery. Mrs. Peterson will show you to the guest suite on the second floor. Let me know if there's anything you need. Anything at all. I want you to be comfortable."

Was it his imagination, or did Katie's eyes widen fractionally as a hint of pink matched her cheeks to her blouse. "Okay."

He cleared his throat. "Take your time settling in. We'll have dinner at seven. If you'd like a drink before that, I'll be in the library."

When Quinten disappeared down the hallway toward the back of the house, Katie exhaled forcefully. She hadn't realized she'd been holding her breath.

The housekeeper, possibly in her late fifties, was pleasant and welcoming as she led Katie up the massive rough wood stairs. She wore a khaki skirt and a white knit shirt. Almost a uniform, but not quite.

"Do you live nearby?" Katie asked.

"Call me Lydia if you like," the other woman said. "Yes. As the crow flies. My husband is a commercial fisherman. The work has its ups and downs. We have a house we love out in the woods, but jobs for me are few and far between. When Mr. Quinten built this house five years ago and advertised for a housekeeper/caretaker, it was the perfect solution."

"That's wonderful. I suppose you don't have to be here full-time since Quin travels frequently."

The housekeeper pointed out a luxurious bathroom and a sitting room with a mini fridge and microwave. "Not as a rule, but since this last surgery, much more often. We've had an in-house physical therapist until very recently. Mr. Quinten is determined to rehab his leg."

"Patience is not his strong suit."

The housekeeper grinned. "You could say that. Mr. Quin has a fully outfitted home gym and has been following the exercise regimen the therapist left behind."

"I see. Do you know where I'll be working?"

"Yes. I can show you in the morning, but not right now. Mr. Quinten was very insistent that you have time to get comfortable and settled. The three brothers worked together last week to rearrange things downstairs. You'll have your own work space. It's not huge, but I think you'll find they've set up everything as closely as possible to what you're used to in Portland."

"Sounds perfect."

"Do you need help with your bags?"

Katie stretched her arms over her head. "Thanks, but no. After all that driving, I could use the exercise."

"Very well. Please let me or Mr. Quinten know if there is anything you need, anything at all."

Katie followed the sturdy woman downstairs and thanked her again before heading out to the car. It took three trips to bring everything inside. She had her favorite pillow, one large suitcase and an assortment of tote bags. Six weeks was a long time. Her books had silently begged to come with her. A personal laptop. Toiletries. And last but not least, a stack of files from Quinten's office. Most everything she needed was online, but there were a few personnel and policy notes that would require Quin's attention.

The house was eerily quiet. Obviously, Mrs. Peterson was still there. She would be preparing dinner. Who knew where Quinten was? His stiff welcome had set Katie's nerves on edge. Neither of them had forgotten how it felt to be naked together. She could see it in his eyes.

She was impressed that Farrell and Zachary had convinced Quin to try this new setup. Quinten Stone was as stubborn and unmalleable as his last name. Sometimes she would swear he disagreed with people just for the heck of it.

When she was done unpacking, she walked out onto the second-floor porch. It ran the length of the house and was furnished with a row of beautiful stained hardwood rocking chairs. She picked her favorite and sat down with a sigh. It was the first time all day she had felt truly relaxed.

True, she still had to get through dinner, but she was working on her positive attitude. Quin was just a man. This was only a job—and a temporary one at that. A woman could cope with anything for six weeks.

The irony of these beautiful rocking chairs moving gently back and forth in the breeze on Quinten's porch wasn't lost on her. The only thing he ever slowed down for was sex. Now that she thought about it, even that was sometimes fast and furious.

Some would call it nervous energy, but Katie knew better. The man was driven. His ability to focus was legendary. He'd won national and international skiing championships so many times he'd been called an iron man on the slopes and in the air at ski jump competitions.

Did he still want to compete?

While they were dating, she had wanted so badly to know the man beneath the mask. She had been intrigued by the rare glimpses into his psyche, flattered by his interest in her. But as time passed, it became clearer and clearer that Quin didn't want anything beyond the physical relationship they shared.

He didn't really want to know her at all.

His indifference had hurt. Would it be the same now?

She dithered over what to wear to dinner. In the end, she didn't change clothes. No reason for him to get the wrong idea. Theirs was to be a working relationship, *not* a meeting of the minds, and especially not a stroll down memory lane.

She did, however, take the time to loosen her hair and brush it out. As soon as the sun went down, the evening would take on a slight chill. The ponytail either seemed too casual for dinner or bared too much of her neck.

All the careful self-lecturing didn't erase her anticipation about the evening to come. Her legs trembled as she descended the stairs and sought out the library. The small, intimate room was filled with floor-to-ceiling bookshelves that overflowed with history, biography and a broad range of fiction.

Quinten *had* changed clothes. He'd been casually dressed during their encounter when she arrived. Now he wore crisp navy trousers and a perfectly starched white button-down shirt. The tortoiseshell glasses that rested on the bridge of his masculine nose as he flipped through a leather-bound volume were new.

She bit down hard on her bottom lip. The man didn't need any help in the sex appeal department. Those studious spectacles were not at all fair to the female sex. "Were these your father's books?" she asked lightly, searching for an innocuous topic as she entered the room. Otherwise, she might simply pounce on him.

The small crease between Quin's masculine eyebrows told her the question puzzled him. "No," he said. "They're mine."

She wasn't quite able to hide her surprise. When did Quinten Stone *ever* sit down long enough to read? "Oh…"

He stared at her, obviously disgruntled. "Did you really think I was nothing but a dumb jock?"

"Of course not," she said. "But you…"

"What?" he demanded. "Spit it out."

What she wanted to say was that he seemed to have changed. That he was somehow more centered than the man she remembered. Perhaps her opinion wouldn't please him. "Nothing," she muttered. "May I have a drink?"

He poured a glass of her favorite champagne and handed it to her. "Cheers," he said gruffly.

Their fingers brushed briefly as he released the flute. How had he remembered this little detail about her preference? "I'm surprised you recalled how much I like this." He must have had a hundred dates since their breakup, been intimate with a dozen women. Isn't that what the Stone men did? Sample the smorgasbord?

Well, maybe not Farrell. As far as Katie could tell, her boss was still in love with his dead wife.

Quinten moved a step closer, though she didn't think he meant to crowd her. His eyes blazed with blue fire. "I remember every moment of our time together, Katie. All of them," he said gruffly. "You're the kind of woman who's hard to forget."

Something about the way he looked at her sucked every atom of oxygen out of the room. Her heartbeat grew sluggish. For one insane moment, she nearly stepped forward into his arms.

"I shouldn't have come, should I?" she whispered raggedly.

"It depends." His gaze settled on her mouth.

"On what?"

"On whether you want to walk back into the fire."

Half an hour later Quinten sat across the table from his new admin and cursed himself for his reckless stupidity. Katie's chocolate-brown eyes were hazy with arousal. That wasn't conceited conjecture on his part. He *knew* her. Intimately. He knew the way she looked when they had shared a night of passion and woke in each other's arms, ready to do it all over again.

Damn it. He hadn't even made it twenty-four hours without stepping over the line. "I'm sorry," he said, the apology both awkward and formal even to his own ears. "I shouldn't have spoken to you that way. You have my word it won't happen again."

Katie stared at him. She had barely touched her roast beef and mashed potatoes. And that was after picking at her Caesar salad. "How can you be so sure?" Her guarded gaze surprised him.

He jerked, physically disturbed by what was surely a teasing question. "Because I won't allow it."

"So pompous, so arrogant." Her gaze seemed to judge him. "We're both adults. And this situation is temporary. Surely we couldn't be faulted for enjoying a temporary liaison."

"I'm not falling for that. You're jerking my chain, aren't you?" Quinten shot a wild glance toward the doorway, expecting at any moment to be rescued from this surreal conversation by the imminently practical Mrs. Peterson.

Good help was hard to find.

"I couldn't resist."

He drained his wine and tried to clear his paper-dry throat. "Still a tease, I see."

Katie ran her thumb up and down the stem of her glass. The sensual gesture was so damned evocative he felt gooseflesh break out all over his body. "I like playing with you, Quin," she said. "Everyone at SRO walks on eggshells around the *boss*. But I know the truth. You're a pussycat when someone rubs your fur the right way." Her mocking smile reached inside his chest and squeezed his heart so hard he ached. But then again, that might be nothing more than raw lust.

"Perhaps we should discuss the work we'll be

doing," he said, still trying to regain control of the situation.

Finally, Mrs. Peterson returned, this time bearing a silver tray with two perfectly torched crème brûlées. "I hope you saved room," she said cheerfully. "This was my grandma's recipe. The custard has been known to make grown men cry."

Katie dug into her dessert with such enthusiasm that Quin felt his forehead bead with sweat. "Omigosh," she moaned. "This is better than sex."

The unflappable housekeeper chuckled. "I won't weigh in on that one, but you two enjoy. I'll clean up the kitchen and let myself out. See you tomorrow morning."

Quin had to force himself to eat the dessert. Not that it wasn't as amazing as Katie had said, but because he was suddenly, stunningly aware of the fact that he was going to be alone in this huge house with the woman he absolutely couldn't take into his bed.

He forced himself to swallow the last bite. "If you'll excuse me, I have to hit the gym and do some exercises." He stood up awkwardly. "Is everything upstairs to your liking?"

He was not running away. Not at all. But he couldn't breathe when he was this close to her.

She stared at him as if she could see inside his brain. "It's lovely," she said. "What time do you want to start in the morning?"

Work, Quin. She's talking about work.

"Mrs. Peterson will have breakfast ready at eight

thirty," he said gruffly. "After we eat, you can bring me up to speed on whatever needs my attention."

"Is there an alarm set tonight?" she asked.

"No. But we're perfectly safe."

"That wasn't why I asked. I didn't want to disturb you if I took a walk later."

He frowned. "I'd rather you not do that alone."

"You just said I'm perfectly safe." She wiped her mouth, tossed her napkin on the table and stood, as well.

His jaw tightened. Other than his brothers, he was not accustomed to people arguing with him. "We get the occasional black bear, and of course, moose. Either or both can be unpredictable."

"I grew up camping out with my parents," Katie said. "I know all the right things to do during an animal encounter."

Quin had the oddest feeling this conversation was about more than any possible danger in the woods. "What if I join you?" he asked impulsively. "Give me an hour."

Her eyes widened. "Can you do that? With your leg?"

Her question piqued his pride. "I'm not an invalid," he snapped. "My leg is one hundred percent healed from the surgery. But soft tissue damage takes longer to get back to normal, at least another six weeks. The doc wants me to be cautious in the meantime."

Katie shook her head slowly, her expression hard to

read. "I can't imagine it. The man who takes chances and flies through the air. Grounded."

He stared at her. "I thought I might get a little sympathy from you."

"Is that what you want from me? Sympathy?"

"I remember you as sweeter, kinder."

"Maybe you hit your head. I'm the same woman I've always been."

Something simmered between them. A sensual awareness that two long years hadn't managed to erase. "An hour," he said. "We'll go for a walk together."

She hesitated so long his stomach clenched.

Finally, she nodded. "Okay. I suppose that's best since I don't know my way around. Wouldn't want to fall into the ocean."

He exhaled. "Good. I'll meet you in the foyer at nine."

Three

Katie changed into her boots and hiking pants and topped them with a thin fleece pullover. Although it was summer, the nights this far north were on the cool side. Since she and Quin weren't tackling a strenuous trail, the extra warmth would feel good.

Her nerves were jittery. Maybe this whole *work-from-Quin's-home* thing was a terrible idea. Had she mentioned the late-night walk in hopes he would want to join her? She couldn't trust her own motives. Her emotions were all over the map. She'd missed Quin. A lot.

From the beginning, being with him had been fun and exciting. One weekend when they were dating, he tried to fly her to Paris for dinner. Katie had declined politely, mildly horrified at the thought of spending all that money on a whim.

Her family was solidly blue-collar. No matter how hard she tried, she couldn't imagine herself assimilating into Quin's jet-set lifestyle. It was possible she had a chip on her shoulder. About fitting in. Years ago, a friend had once called her a reverse snob for judging her wealthy bosses without really knowing them. The comment had stung, because it contained a grain of truth.

As pleasant as it had been to have a man like Quin shower her with attention and lavish her with gifts, she didn't need all those things to be happy. What she liked about Quin wasn't his money—it was *him*. But it seemed to her that he had used the expensive presents as a shield, a way to keep her at arm's length. She could never get through to him with a meaningful, genuine connection.

At five till nine she scooted down the stairs. He was waiting for her at the bottom looking darkly handsome and brooding. "Do you want to see the water?" he asked. "The moon is full. Should be a good view."

"Sounds wonderful."

Exiting the house was awkward. There was a moment when she was sure he was going to take her arm or link his fingers with hers. In the old days that would have been normal. Now, not so much.

Quin kept a hand resting on the stair rail as they descended. For a man who'd had his entire knee replaced six weeks ago, he moved with impressive grace. But she knew that an elite athlete wouldn't take kindly to the limitations of his current situation.

"We'll take a trail through the woods," he said. "It meanders a bit, but it's been cleared, and it's easy to follow even in the dark."

"Sounds good."

The path, strewn with pine needles and last autumn's leaves, was wide enough for two people to walk side by side. Here in the great outdoors—enveloped in the peace of a quiet summer evening—Katie felt a huge, poignant sadness for all she had lost. She couldn't *make* Quin be the man she wanted him to be.

As long as she reminded herself that he wasn't part of her future, perhaps she could get through this six weeks unscathed. Her heart clenched with regret. For a moment, she wasn't sure which she missed the most, the friend or the lover. Was it possible to resurrect the friendship and avoid the temptation to tumble back into his bed?

The fact that her pulse was all over the map said no.

Eventually, the trail led out of the woods into a clearing.

"Watch your step," Quin said. "We're close to the edge."

Just ahead was nothing but darkness, although the moon was full and bright. The pitch-black ocean was an unknown expanse. A little tingle worked its way down Katie's spine.

She had a love/hate relationship with water. After almost drowning in a neighbor's pool when she was seven, she had always struggled to enjoy getting *in* the water. On the other hand, she was more than happy to sit and watch the tides go in and out.

Now that she and Quin were away from the trees, she could hear the crash of the sea on the shore below. This part of the coastline wasn't immensely high. Even so, the rocky promontory where Quin had built his house commanded a stunning view. She had glimpsed it on her arrival. She would enjoy the sea for as long as she was here.

Tonight, though, was different. Quinten had led her to the edge of certainty. The brink of safety. She shivered and wrapped her arms around her waist. Her stomach flipped and flopped with excitement or fear or a combination of both.

Their silent contemplation was not entirely comfortable. The rifts between them were gone but not forgotten. Quin was still an enigma. And Katie still wanted a man who would love her in a forever kind of way.

Since Quin wasn't likely to change, maybe this was a chance for Katie to find closure and learn how to relate to him in a new way.

She touched his arm briefly, barely making contact. "Will you tell me about the car accident?" she asked.

At her side, she felt his posture stiffen. His voice was low and gravelly when he responded. "I don't remember much. The doctors say I may never recover those moments. All I know is that Dad and I had a driver that day. We'd been visiting Farrell up here and were headed back to Portland. Somewhere east of Bangor, another vehicle crossed the center line and hit us head-on. My father was killed instantly when he was thrown from the car. No seat belt. My side of the car took the brunt of the collision. My right leg was crushed."

"Oh, Quin. I'm so sorry."

He shrugged. "I've had surgery, more than once actually. Pins. Reconstruction. You can imagine. Finally, they said they had done all they could."

"And then?"

"I convinced myself I had to get back out on the slopes. It was stupid, I know, but I was desperate. Skiing is my life."

"But you crashed."

He chuckled, though there was no real amusement in the sound. "Crashed and burned, you might say. I didn't go back to square one. Instead, I fell backward at least a hundred miles. The leg was so jacked up this time that a replacement was my only option."

"And the skiing?"

His profile was beautiful and remote in the moonlight. "No one knows."

They stood there, both contemplating those three awful words. She couldn't imagine Quin not being able to glide down a black diamond slope. "It must have been even harder grieving your father in the midst of all that," Katie said.

He moved restlessly, likely because his leg was hurting. "Surely you remember my father's reputation. He wasn't an easy man."

"I knew how people talked about him at work, but with his sons…" She trailed off, not quite knowing how to express what she wanted to say. *Mrs.* Stone had died when Quentin was born. The boys had been raised by their father and his drill sergeant brand of parenting.

Katie had her own issues with Quinten's stern parent, but now was not the time to rehash old wounds.

Quin shoved his hands in his pockets and kicked a small stone over the edge. "I loved my father, I suppose. I didn't want him to die. But the business is a lot easier now that it's just the three of us."

Katie had always been able to read people. It was one of her gifts, and one that wasn't always pleasant. Right now, she could tell that Quin was hurting, physically *and* mentally. She wanted to comfort him, to bring back his rakish smile and devil-may-care personality.

But any move on her part to initiate physical contact, no matter how innocent, would escalate rapidly. She and Quin shared a powerful attraction, even now, after two years apart. It shimmered in the air between them, almost tangible.

"We should go," she said, suddenly aware of the danger in this late-night walk. "I was up early this morning. I'm beat."

Quin nodded slowly. "Of course."

They didn't speak as they reversed their course. All her excitement about seeing Quin again had coalesced into a painful knot in her stomach, mostly

because she had stood at this exact emotional preci-
pice before.

It was like eating six cones of cotton candy at the
county fair. The crazy choice was fun and deliciously
indulgent at the time, but always ended up hurting
you in the end.

Back at the house, they climbed the stairs. When
Quin unlocked the door and stepped aside, Katie
brushed past him, only to pause in the foyer. "Good
night, Quin," she said.

For a fleeting moment, his guard slipped. She saw
the hunger in his gaze. The intensity of it lodged a
lump in her throat. Long seconds passed during which
she was absolutely certain he was going to kiss her.

Instead, after breathless moments, he caressed her
cheek with the back of his hand, his hard fingers
warm against her chilled chin. "I'm glad you're here,
Katie. Good night."

Then he turned his back and walked away.

Katie had trouble falling asleep, despite her fatigue. When she'd agreed to this unorthodox plan,
it was under the misguided notion that she had mas-
tered her infatuation with Quinten Stone. Apparently,
she was as prone as her ex-lover to making dumb
decisions.

She wanted to jump back in her car and escape
to Portland.

The night was long and not particularly restful.

When morning came, she felt hungover and appre-
hensive. Was it possible that Quin read her as easily

as she did him? Did he know how much she wanted him still?

Over breakfast, neither of them said much. Mrs. Peterson interrupted the uncomfortable silences, bustling in and out with fresh coffee, additional hot biscuits and second helpings of eggs and bacon.

At one point, Katie leaned forward and whispered to Quin. "I usually eat yogurt and granola at home."

He lifted an eyebrow. "Are you complaining?"

"Heavens, no."

The quick exchange lightened the mood.

Finally, the wonderful meal was over, and Quin showed her the makeshift office setup. All the amenities were there. The only eyebrow-raising moment was seeing how close his desk was to hers in the small converted downstairs bedroom.

Shoving aside a host of inappropriate emotions, Katie turned on the top-of-the-line laptop and uploaded the files she had brought via flash drive from Portland. "I'll email some things to you," she said. "A lot of it has to do with the first and second quarter financial reports. Zachary wants you to look over them, and then Farrell needs you to sign off on some preliminary designs."

After that, the morning settled into a routine. With both of them busy—independently but in the same close quarters—it might have been awkward. Fortunately, once Katie immersed herself in work, the hours flew rapidly.

She and Quinten were just getting ready to head

to the dining room for lunch when Zachary showed up in the doorway.

Quin frowned. "I thought you were in Portland."

"I was. Now I'm here. I brought the chopper." He glanced at Katie. "Have you told her yet?"

"Haven't had a chance. She only arrived yesterday afternoon. We've spent this morning getting up to speed on everything I've missed."

Katie looked from one brother to the other. "Told me what? That sounds ominous."

Zachary perched on the corner of her desk, one leg swinging. "You could say that. We're starting to believe that Stone River Outdoors has been the target of corporate espionage."

Her eyes widened. "You can't be serious."

"Unfortunately, we are," Zachary said. "I've stumbled across irregularities in a few of our accounts. Farrell has seen a couple of his most promising ideas pop up in the marketplace. The first time, we wrote it off as coincidence. After all, two people can have the same idea at roughly the same moment. But then it happened again."

It was Katie's turn to frown. "Why didn't Farrell tell me any of this?"

"He's been trying to keep it under the radar to see if anyone at SRO tips his or her hand. Plus, we didn't want to place you in danger."

"Danger?" Katie laughed until she realized that Quentin and Zachary weren't the slightest bit amused.

Zachary spoke up again. "Farrell and I started to

wonder if the crash that killed Dad and injured Quin was not an accident at all."

She sucked in a sharp breath, her gaze darting to Quinten. He'd barely said a word. "And what do *you* think?" she asked.

He ground his jaw. "That's the hell of it. I was recovering from the crash, so I wasn't dialed into what was happening. The guys didn't want to worry me when I was having my leg pieced back together. And then, of course, I pulled my dumbass stunt out on the ski slopes."

Zachary winced. "Yeah. A few weeks ago, we told Quin everything. It's true the doctor wants him to take it easy. A side benefit of having you here, though, is that you and Quin can take a look at all the departments remotely and see if you notice any unusual activity or red flags."

Katie gnawed her lip. "I understand how Farrell's department runs. That's my baby. Quinten controls a whole lot of stuff I know nothing about."

"I can teach you," Quinten said. "You're one of the smartest people I know."

Zachary nodded. "Quin is right. Plus, you're an outsider, so you might notice something the three of us have missed."

"I can't believe this," Katie said. "It sounds like a spy movie."

Quentin stood and waved them all toward lunch. "We hope we're wrong. We hope we're just being paranoid. The evidence is piling up, though. Somebody may be trying to take down Stone River Outdoors."

Over corned beef sandwiches and thick wedges of watermelon, Katie took a quieter role as the two brothers joked and laughed and eventually dedicated themselves to serious business. Zachary knew Mrs. Peterson, of course. When he teased her, the older woman's cheeks turned pink.

Even a stranger could see that Zachary and Quinten were clearly siblings. They shared the same broad shoulders and lanky build. But Zachary's eyes were brown, and his hair was chestnut. He probably inherited his coloring from his mother.

There were personality differences, too. Quinten was intense, competitive. Zachary climbed mountains and was also an incredibly athletic man, but he bounced from one activity to the next—whether it was racing sport cars in Abu Dhabi or navigating the Amazon in search of new experiences.

Zachary popped the top on his second beer. "This will be it for me. I still have to fly back to Portland later."

Quinten lifted an eyebrow. "I thought you'd be spending the night." He glanced at Katie. "My brother's house makes my place look like a shack in the woods."

"He exaggerates." Zach grinned. "But it is pretty damned awesome. I'll show you around sometime," he said to Katie.

A change in Quin's expression told Katie he didn't like that idea. Maybe because his middle brother had a reputation for playing the field—a *large* field. She smiled at Zachary. "I'd love to see your home when you have a chance. And what about Farrell's?"

Quin relaxed visibly. "Farrell has the biggest chunk

of land…his choice. It starts at the ocean and runs in-land, narrower than what Zach and I have, but long. From the air, our houses aren't that far apart along the coastline. When we're in the mood, we can even walk from one to the next."

Katie nodded. "And yours is the farthest south, be-cause I didn't see the others as I drove in."

Zachary interrupted before Quin could respond. "Yep. It's the whole birth order thing. Farrell's is first, or northernmost if you like. Then me in the middle. And Quin, here, brings up the rear."

Quin made a rude gesture.

Katie laughed. "I thought middle children were supposed to be the peacemakers."

Zachary shrugged. "I never did like people telling me who I was expected to be, whether it was a book or my *dearly departed, God-rest-his-soul* father."

After a beat of silence following Zachary's unex-pectedly revealing comment, Katie folded her nap-kin and scooted back in her chair and stood. "I want to help, any way I can."

The brothers rose to their feet in unison. "You al-ready are," Quin said. "The three of us couldn't think of a single other person more capable of helping out with our situation than you."

Zachary shook her hand. "Thanks again, Katie." He grabbed his keys and phone from a nearby table. "Let me know if anything comes up."

Four

Let me know if anything comes up.

Zachary's parting words echoed in Quentin's head for days. He knew Zachary was referring to possible clues about espionage, but where Quentin's mind went was a whole different ball game.

It was only the second week of Katie's intrusion into his routine, and already Quin felt out of sorts. His brothers had been extremely generous in not berating him for the time he'd been away from work. They had shouldered the burden of his responsibilities and had kept things running. That additional load meant his siblings had been tied down far more than usual.

Now it was Quin's turn to deal with important company issues and let Zach and Farrell get back to what they did best.

Unfortunately, that meant Quin had to utilize Katie's considerable talents. Now that she was here, under his roof, he wasn't sure he could handle it. Though he had no residual animosity about the way their relationship ended, it would be a foolish mistake—on several counts—to let personal feelings and urges creep back in.

Katie was an employee of Stone River Outdoors. An employee at the highest level. It didn't matter that he still responded to her physically. She was off-limits. Not only that, but she had made it very clear two years ago—he wasn't the kind of man she wanted in her life on a permanent basis.

He couldn't fault her logic. He was a selfish bastard. He'd put his desire to pit himself against the ski slopes ahead of what was good for his family. Now he had to deal with the consequences.

At this particular moment, he was taking a break from the claustrophobic in-home office on the pretext of stretching his muscles. Katie had worked quietly all morning, barely paying any attention to him at all. Didn't matter. All he could think about was dragging her down the hall and into his bed.

After a cycle of reps on the rowing machine that left him sweaty but still restless, he moved to the leg press. His range of motion improved daily. For any normal person, the speed and breadth of his recovery would be cause for celebration.

But Quin had never been satisfied with *normal* or ordinary. He'd spent years in search of *extraordinary*. Better, stronger, faster.

If he wasn't an award-winning skier, then who was he? The business didn't count. Heading up Stone River Outdoors was what he did, not who he was.

Unfortunately, the tenets that applied to being an elite athlete didn't translate to relationships. He'd never known his mother. Though he was tight with his siblings, he had no sisters. His father had governed their family life with authoritarian might. Any inkling of softer emotions had been beaten out of the Stone boys with a belt or a paddle.

Quin had suffered more than he needed to, because he was stubborn and wouldn't give his father the satisfaction of seeing him cry. Maybe he was screwed from the beginning when it came to understanding the female sex. He didn't have much to offer any woman in the way of emotional intimacy, which was why his romantic liaisons tended toward the brief and expedient. He couldn't *train* for the kind of closeness women wanted.

Katie had been the first female to make him wonder whether he had it in him to fall in love. And look how that had turned out.

He cursed as more sweat rolled into his eyes. This was nuts. He was letting her presence in his house disrupt his recovery. She was temporary. There was no going back to the past.

Only because he refused to be a coward did he shower and return to the office down the hall.

Katie looked up with a smile. "Oh good. I had a pile of questions and couldn't go much further without your input."

How could she be so damned *happy* all the time? Did she really feel none of the desperate need that was consuming him from the inside out?

Ten minutes later Quin found himself sitting elbow to elbow with his former lover, the two of them poring over reports and data that had to be reconciled and disseminated to the appropriate department heads.

Every time he leaned in to check a figure or answer a question, he inhaled her familiar scent. Like one of Pavlov's dogs, he salivated inwardly, his body on high alert. His enforced celibacy, combined with the advent of this extraordinary woman into his monastic existence, made him horny and desperate and despairing.

How was he going to survive an entire six weeks without pouncing on her? It wasn't a pretty picture.

Katie, on the other hand, barely seemed to notice he was around. She arose early in the mornings and went jogging through the forest. After that, he could hear her showering upstairs. Memories of what she looked like slick and wet tormented him.

When she arrived at the breakfast table every day, they made mundane conversation over their meal and then headed to the office and settled in to work. The teasing, flirtatious woman who sparred with him in the very beginning had disappeared. Perhaps, like Quinten, she had decided that the job at hand was more important than revisiting an old relationship.

By the beginning of week three, he'd had enough. If he didn't get out of this house soon, he was going to expire from cabin fever.

When he found his temporary admin, she was in the process of scanning and emailing quality control reports to an independent contractor who would be visiting their manufacturing plant in a couple of months.

Katie glanced up at him. "Farrell called the landline. He said you weren't answering your cell."

Guilt assailed Quin. He'd been ignoring his phone all morning. "Anything urgent?"

She wrinkled her nose. "I think they worry about you."

He felt his face heat. "I'm not a child. I'm in charge of the whole damn company."

"I know that, Quin. They do, too. But you almost died, and you've had to give up something you love, at least temporarily. That would be a lot for anyone to handle, plus you lost your dad, as well."

He scowled. "I won't be smothered. I won't do anything else stupid, I swear. But I won't be smothered."

She nodded slowly. "Okay. Would it be better if I gave you a break? I could go home and come back in a week."

The thought startled him. "God, no. You're not the problem. But I had an idea, and I was hoping you would agree."

Now her stance was wary. "What kind of an idea?"

"Zachary has Broadway tickets to see *Hamilton* in New York this weekend with one of his interchangeable girlfriends. His date is ill, and he says he doesn't want to look for a replacement on such short notice. Farrell mentioned to him that you're a history buff, so they thought you might like to see the musical. With me," Quin clarified.

"Oh." Her cheeks flushed. "I've never been to New York. Always wanted to. How would we get there?"

"I'm not cleared to fly the jet yet, but I can hire a pilot to take us down and back. We'd have two hotel rooms, of course. You'd need something fancy for both evenings, and then casual wear in case we decide to go walking in Central Park. We can do some shopping if you'd like."

She stared at him so long he had to fight the urge to fidget. "Quin?" she said.

"What?"

"Is this a ploy to seduce me?"

"Absolutely not." He bristled. "I do occasionally think of other people besides myself. I wanted you to have some fun."

"Calm down. I appreciate the sentiment, but you're not stupid. You have to know I still want you."

His jaw dropped before he caught himself and snapped it shut. "You do?" he said hoarsely.

"Of course I do. You're a handsome man. We share a past. We're here together in this enormous house with no distractions. Believe me, though, if we ever decide we want to end up in bed again, it will have *nothing* to do with work. Are we clear?" Her challenging stare made his spine tingle.

"Yes, ma'am. Does that mean you're up for a weekend in the big city?"

"I love the idea," she said. "Let's do it."

* * *

Katie was in big trouble. She'd been striving to maintain a business-as-usual attitude while working with Quin. If he was going to whisk her away to one of the most romantic cities in the world, she might forget to protect her heart. But still she'd said yes. She wanted to be with him too badly to say no.

For the first time, she seriously pondered the implications of sleeping with him again. She was older and wiser now than the last time they'd dated. But she still wanted something that was out of reach. She wanted him to *need* her. Desperately. Not for a momentary sexual encounter, but in every way that a man could need a woman.

She was clear that she had made the right choice before. He cared more about skiing than he did about Katie or any woman. The truth hurt. And then there was the money thing. She and Quinten Stone didn't come from different worlds; they came from opposite planets.

Breaking up with him two years ago had been the sensible thing to do.

Most people she knew worried about how often they could hit Starbucks each week without blowing their monthly food budgets. Quentin bought champagne like it was tap water.

His emotional distance and his careless attitude toward money bothered her still.

The big question was—could she let herself indulge in this once-in-a-lifetime trip and not end up sleeping with him? The temptation would be there, undoubtedly. Soon, Quin would no longer require her professional assistance. On a finite day and time in the near future, her work in his home would be done.

When Quinten was cleared to return to Portland and resume his full roster of responsibilities, Katie would be free to go back to her role as second in command of the R & D department as Farrell's right-hand woman.

That day was still a few weeks away. What about all the lovely unpredictable moments in between?

For the remaining forty-eight hours until their departure, Quin made himself scarce. Katie buried herself in work. She was forced to email Quin her questions, because the frustrating man was tucked away somewhere in this big, lonely house.

By the time Friday morning rolled around, Katie's mix of anxiety and excitement rose to fever pitch. She had asked Quinten if they could stop in Portland and let her grab a few things she needed for the weekend. He had vehemently refused, insisting that she was on the company dime at the moment and that the CEO's expense account would more than cover the cost of a *couple of cocktail dresses*.

He said that last bit dismissively, as if couture clothing was little more expensive than the price of a yoga top and pants or a college T-shirt. To him, it probably was.

At last, they were on the plane and airborne. Katie tried not to gawk. Two years ago, she hadn't been Quin's girlfriend long enough to warrant a journey in this sleek, utterly luxurious Cirrus Vision Jet. It was light and fast and nimble, the perfect vehicle for a fantasy weekend.

Quin talked to the pilot for a few minutes before returning to his seat beside hers. From the tiny built-in fridge at his side, he extracted two mini bottles of wine and a cellophane-wrapped tray of cheese, fruit and crackers.

"Have some," he urged. "LaGuardia may be busy. Who knows how long it will be till lunch."

"We just ate breakfast," she protested. But still she took the glass he offered her, along with a selection of snacks.

The jet had large windows. The day was blue and bright. Nothing to fear, even for a novice traveler. It seemed as if they were gliding on clouds.

The wine must have given her Dutch courage. They'd been aloft less than an hour when she blurted out a question. "Is this how you feel when you're flying down a mountain?"

He actually winced. For a moment, she glimpsed his raw grief. "You could say that," he said, his shoulders hunched. "It's the quiet and the freedom. I've never found anything else like it."

After his painfully truthful answer, she was sorry she had brought it up. She didn't want him to be sad. And she didn't want to remind herself that skiing gave him something she couldn't.

Today, he looked every inch the successful billionaire. His sport coat and slacks were perfectly tailored, drawing attention to his fit, muscular body. He'd brought along those tortoiseshell reading glasses. The ones that made her all gooey inside with lust.

"I never knew you wore glasses," she said. "When did that happen?"

"During all those surgeries, it was too complicated to fool with contacts. I got these, and now it's a habit, I guess. I see fine at a distance, but farsightedness runs in the family. Or maybe it was all those years of squinting into snow glare—who knows?"

All Katie knew was that she had a burning desire to see him naked in bed reading the *Wall Street Journal* with nothing but those sexy frames perched on his masculine nose.

They landed in New York and handled the formalities without issue. A private car met them as soon as they were done. Katie had a hard time not gawking. The traffic and the iconic yellow cabs and the tall buildings. Everywhere she looked, the city hummed and buzzed with activity.

The trip from the airport into the city was slow. She had plenty of time to drool over sidewalk flower shops, tiny art galleries, and eventually, on Madison Avenue, the glitzy storefronts of every high-end retail name in the world.

Quin had booked them rooms at the Carlyle on the Upper East Side. Katie adored the building on sight. She knew enough of the glamorous address to remember that Princess Diana had been known to stay here. The iconic hotel was only a block from the park and five blocks from the Met.

The bellman took them up to adjoining rooms on

the thirty-second floor. With the drapes open wide, the view of Central Park was breathtaking. When the uniformed employee departed to deposit Quin's suitcase in his room, Katie threw her arms around her ex-lover and gave him a quick hug. "My first trip to New York. Thank you, Quin. This is incredible."

His pleased smile told her he was glad she was impressed. "Shopping next," he promised. "Or maybe lunch first."

"How about a hot dog vendor?" Katie asked. "I've always wanted to do that. And sit on a bench in the sun? What do you think?"

He gave her a wry look. "You won't find any hot dog vendors in this rarified neighborhood. But I might be able to dig up a gourmet pizza place. Would that do?"

Over thick, tomatoey slices of cheesy goodness, Katie relaxed. Maybe she and Quin would have sex during this trip, and maybe they wouldn't. She had a bad habit of overthinking things. As a self-confessed type A control freak, surely she could try to relax and see how the weekend unfolded.

It wouldn't hurt her to loosen up a little.

When she and Quin were dating, they had argued about money a lot. She thought he threw his fortune away too easily, and Quin said Katie let her relatives sponge off her to an alarming extent.

To Katie, money was something a person shared and spread around to do good. Her parents had struggled to get by, but they had helped their neighbors. In Katie's eyes, Quin—having the Stone fortune at his disposal—should have been a philanthropist.

In Quin's defense, though, Katie had to admit she didn't have healthy boundaries with the people she loved. As the only person of her extended family to have gone to college, she had ended up comfortably well off while her siblings and cousins lived paycheck to paycheck. Whenever she felt guilty for her blessings, she invariably let herself be manipulated into giving out loans that somehow were never repaid.

The hugest fight she and Quin ever had happened not long before she broke up with him. She had innocently asked his advice about rehab programs. When he questioned her, she admitted she was thinking about paying for her sister's boyfriend to go into a treatment facility.

Quin had been both furious and incredulous. He pointed out that the boyfriend—who had been in and out of jail—was never likely to agree, and if he did, he wouldn't last the course.

Katie called Quin callous. He'd told her she was naive and credulous. The bitter quarrel had colored what was left of their time together.

And then his father had intervened, and Katie's humiliation had been complete.

Five

Quin had made the best of his *passenger* status on the jet, but he hated not being the one at the controls. It helped having Katie along.

He'd gotten a kick out of watching her face today as they traveled. She was bubbling over with excitement and not afraid to show it. Her enthusiasm for life was one of the qualities that had drawn him to her in the beginning. That and her limber, soft body.

The memories made him sweat.

Now, while he finished his pizza, he studied her again. She looked beautiful as always. Her pale blond hair was loose around her shoulders. Subtle eye shadow made her beautiful brown eyes sparkle. With her tailored black jacket and pants and a tangerine silk blouse, she looked as if she belonged among the throngs of Manhattan professional women out for lunch.

At the moment, Katie was chatting up their waiter. Quin watched as the handsome young man grew more animated. Katie coaxed him to talk about his theatrical dreams and how he missed his family back in Kansas. After three trips to the table for drink refills, fresh parmesan and extra napkins, the kid was halfway in love with Quin's date.

It was nothing sexual that Katie did. She was simply Katie being Katie. The interest she showed in other people was genuine and authentic. Her sunny personality drew both men and women into her orbit. Everyone wanted to be her friend.

And Katie had said that *she* still wanted Quin.

The admission rocked him to the core. He was pretty sure she regretted saying it. If she still wanted him physically, why in the hell had they broken up? They had so much chemistry between them. Did she not realize that such an intense attraction was rare and wonderful?

Two years ago, she had wanted more from him. He knew it. And he resented the way she was always pressuring him to be a better man. What if the man he was didn't get any better? What if being selfish was his default setting?

He'd had his share of casual sex before Katie came along. Even a handful of what he would characterize as *serious* relationships. None of those women had kept him up nights wondering, wanting, wishing he could reset the clock and rewrite the past.

When Katie had given him the heave-ho, he'd been embarrassingly shocked. He'd thought they were doing great. How could he have been so blind to what was happening? He'd felt like a fool.

If it had been only his ego that had taken a hit, he probably would have brushed it off and taken his dismissal like a man. But he'd been so dazzled by Katie and drowning in raging lust, it had literally never occurred to him that the relationship was in danger.

Now, memories of the playful passion they once shared made him itchy and horny and desperate. Katie said she still wanted him, but what did that mean? If they were to resume a physical relationship, it would be on his terms this time.

At last, his patience for seeing another man flirt with Katie ran out. "We should go," he said abruptly. "That is if you want time to pick up a few things for the weekend." He held out his platinum card to the waiter.

When the kid disappeared, Katie gave Quin a placating smile. "I wouldn't feel comfortable in any of these Madison Avenue stores. I brought several tops to swap out with what I have on now. And I threw in some running clothes and shoes. One of my friends at home came to a Broadway show recently. She told me you see people in jeans and sneakers all the way up to fancy stuff. I'll be fine without anything new."

Quin ground his teeth. The one sure thing he could offer Katie was pampering. He could wine and dine her and shower her with gifts. But the frustrating woman didn't want his money. She had told him so on more than one occasion. How could they connect if she continually dismissed his strengths? Extravagance was his strong suit—that and hot sex. Katie was honest about wanting him. The rest of it didn't seem to matter to her.

He debated his options. "I brought a tux for this evening," he said. "But I can buy a suit to wear if it would make you more comfortable."

Her eyes widened, aghast. "Don't buy a new suit. I'm sure you have half a dozen or more at home."

"Fine. I won't buy a suit. But let's dress up and have fun tonight," he cajoled. "It won't hurt, I promise. Stone River Outdoors can afford to buy a valuable employee a little black dress."

She chewed her lip. Hard. He could see the hesitation in her body language and in her eyes. "I don't know…"

"No strings attached. I swear."

When she swallowed, he saw the muscles in her delicate throat ripple. "I can't even imagine what a dress like that will cost," she said. "I don't like pushy, condescending salesclerks. They intimidate me."

Quin chuckled. "One of Zach's old girlfriend's works three blocks from here. I sent her a text earlier and told her we might drop by after lunch. She promised to pull a few things out of stock for you, so it won't take forever. Her name is Katiya. She's Bulgarian, I think. You'll like her."

Katie scowled. "Did you date her after Zach did? Is that why you're so chummy?"

He held up his hands. "Wow. Suspicious much?

My brothers and I don't share lady friends. Zachary and Katiya spent a lot of time in Maine, so I know her pretty well."

"Fine. We'll go see her. But if she doesn't have anything appropriate, I don't want to spend the whole day shopping. It's my first time in New York. You promised me the Met."

"So I did." He nodded in surrender, wanting to laugh, but knowing it wasn't the moment. Just then, his phone dinged. The text made him smile. He showed it to Katie. "Zach and Farrell are in Midtown for a meeting. They want to know if we'd like to have dinner with them before they fly back to Portland. We don't have to," he added quickly. "We can wait until after the show." Truthfully, he wasn't entirely sure he wanted his aggravating brothers horning in on his night out with Katie. Still, having two chaperones might keep him from doing something recklessly stupid.

Katie hunched her shoulders and looked around her as if someone might be listening to their conversation. "I know it's probably incredibly unsophisticated," she whispered, "but I *hate* the idea of eating a big meal at ten thirty at night. Tell them yes. We'd love to."

"Even if it has to be early? Entering the theater after the lights go down is frowned upon."

"Whenever you say," she said. "It will be fun getting to know Zachary better."

Quin chewed on that unpleasant thought. Women loved Zachary. Come to think of it, Zach and Katie probably *would* hit it off. Katie never met a stranger, and Zach had been charming females since he was in kindergarten.

Before Quin could resolve his unease, someone held the door open for them and they stepped out onto the sidewalk, blinded by the July sunshine and a blast of heat. New York City in the summer could be rainy or brutally hot. Quin would take the heat any day, but he didn't know about his companion.

"Shall I get a cab?" he asked, moving toward the curb.

Katie grabbed his arm. "You said it was only three blocks. Let's walk." She paused, visibly stricken. "Unless your knee is bothering you. I'm sorry. I wasn't thinking."

Again, Quin ground his jaw. "Good Lord, Kat. I can stroll down the damned street. Come on. It's this way."

In his frustration, he had shortened her name without thinking. The affectionate *Kat* was what he had called her in the midst of their wild affair. Did she even notice his slip?

They headed off along the sunbaked sidewalk, dodging other pedestrians. Katie didn't say a word, her expression subdued. She had shed her jacket. Her bare arms were slender and defined with attractive muscles. Did she work out? It occurred to him that many aspects of her life were a mystery to him. Their time together had been relatively brief and more focused on sex than standard getting-to-know-you dates.

When they arrived at the well-known French fashion house, Katie almost balked again. "Couldn't we try something a little less pricey?"

He opened the plate glass door with the gold lettering and steered her inside. The cool air-conditioned air washed over them like a benediction. "Quit worrying. As thrifty as you are, you'll probably still be wearing this same dress a dozen years from now. Do the amortization. You're good at math. It will make you feel better."

Katiya sauntered up to greet them, her slender feet clad in five-inch heels that made Katie's eyes widen. "Quin," Katiya said, smiling broadly. She kissed him on both cheeks. "It's been too long. I was sorry to hear about your father. And your leg." She looked him over. "You seem to be doing well."

Quin returned the kisses. "I'm great. This is a friend of mine, Katie Duncan. We came to the city on short notice, and she needs a dress. Broadway show. Dinner with Farrell and Zachary. You know the deal."

Katiya kissed Katie on both cheeks, as well. "I have exactly the thing. Since dear Quin gave me a *heads*-up—I think that's the expression—I had time to pick and choose. The weather is hot as Hades this weekend. I thought perhaps plenty of bare skin."

Quin nodded soberly. "Bare skin. I like it already."

Katie punched his arm. "Go read your email."

"Yes, ma'am."

Katiya gave him an arch smile. "We'll be in the back. There's coffee and champagne and treats. Make yourself at home."

* * *

Katie trailed behind the gorgeous woman with the jet-black hair and felt her self-esteem plummet. *This* was the kind of female Stone men dated. Glamorous. Worldly. Fabulously dressed.

The jacket and pants Katie wore were from the clearance rack. With an extra coupon.

As Katiya swooshed open the thick damask curtain of a spacious fitting room, Katie couldn't contain her curiosity. "So how long were you and Zachary together?"

The woman who must have been a model at one point in her life shot a tiny smile over her elegant shoulder. "Not quite a year. It was a long time ago. We decided we were better off as friends." Katiya held up her left hand. "After that, I met the most wonderful history professor at NYU and married him six months later."

A history professor? "Congratulations," Katie said.

"Thank you. He is my soulmate. What can I say? True love is wonderful." The saleswoman waved Katie into the little nook. "Strip down to your undies. I'll grab what we need."

Back at the hotel, Katie had some kick-ass new underwear in her suitcase. Just in case. The fact that she had taken it to Maine meant her subconscious was more honest than she was.

Today, though, she wore solid white cotton. Too bad. She wished she had known that Quin meant for them to shop for a dress immediately. She would like to have worn something more upscale. Too late now.

Katiya returned with an armful of black. "I brought long and above-the-knee both. Either will be appropriate. It's your personal preference. Try this halter dress first, though. You have the figure to pull it off, and in the heat, you'll be glad you're mostly naked. I'll leave the rest of them on this hook just outside the cubicle. If you need me, press the button."

Mostly naked? Katie gulped. She took the dress the other woman handed her and examined it at arm's length. The black crepe fabric was light as air and had a lovely, subtle crinkle pattern. No bra with this one.

She was down to her bikini panties. Though she had been hot before, now she shivered in the extremely efficient air-conditioning. Or maybe her tremors were the result of anticipation about the evening ahead. She was torn in two opposing directions. Throw caution to the wind and sleep with Quinten Stone? Or play it safe and not make the same mistake twice.

When she slipped the gown over her head, it fell like a whisper to her ankles. The design of the dress left her shoulders bare, as promised. But it also plunged to the base of her spine in back and halfway to her navel in the front. *Good grief.* Where was a sweater when you needed one?

Katiya appeared without warning. She peeked through the curtain. "How do you think?"

The odd expression was endearing. Katie inhaled and glanced at herself in the mirror. She wrinkled her nose. "I do like it. But this is a lot of bare skin. A. Lot."

The other woman chuckled. "You look stunning."

She put her hands on Katie's waist. "See how it slides over your curves? This is one time when small breasts are a plus."

Katie loved her reflection in the mirror. The couture gown made her feel like the proverbial million bucks. But she didn't have the courage to wear this in front of Quin. How could she? He would take this sensual dress as an outright invitation.

"Let me try the others," she said.

Katiya shook her head vehemently. "I wouldn't be doing my job if I let you walk away from this choice. It's perfection. You know I'm right."

"I suppose." Katie smoothed her hands over her flat stomach, already imagining the expression on Quin's face when he saw her in this.

"Will you need shoes and a clutch?" Katiya asked.

Katie pondered the possibility of finding a discount store in this zip code. "I suppose so."

It took another half hour to select accessories and jewelry. Even the *costume* stuff was outrageously expensive. Some of the necklaces cost more than Katie's monthly rent.

Apparently, Katiya and Quin had been communicating via text. Before Katie could lodge a further protest, the steamroller saleswoman had swaddled the new dress in layers of tissue and tucked it into a glossy shopping bag—on top of the shoebox.

The jewelry, safely stowed in a mauve linen drawstring bag, nestled in a deep corner. Katiya had already arranged to have Katie's purchases delivered to the hotel.

Katie put on her own clothes again, feeling alarmingly out of her element. This fantasy shopping spree was delightful, but it gave her an odd feeling under the circumstances. The hour of decision was fast approaching.

Why had she told Quin she still wanted him? Was her subconscious trying to force the issue? Did she *want* Quin to play the role of seducer? It seemed more honest to simply admit she would like to sleep with him again. As he had said earlier—*no strings attached*.

Truthfully, she wanted strings. Lots of them. She wanted Quin to care about the things she cared about—to woo her in a way that said he understood her discomfort with his money. That said he understood her. Was that even possible?

Her time with Quin was half over already. Soon, she would be back in her pleasant condo in Portland, going about her ordinary routine. She might see him now and again in passing, but their day-to-day lives wouldn't intersect. Her six-week stint in the Maine woods would be only a memory.

If she said yes tonight, could she be satisfied with so much less than she yearned for?

Back at the front of the store, Quin and Katiya had their heads together, deep in conversation.

Quin looked up when Katie approached. "What? No fashion show?"

His lazy grin lit a spark in her belly. Her legs trembled. "Get over yourself," she said. "That's old-school cinema. You're not Richard Gere, and I'm not Julia Roberts."

His eyebrows raised in tandem. "I should hope not. We Stone men may have our faults, but doing the Pygmalion thing with charming hookers isn't one of them." Her comment had apparently insulted him.

"I was kidding," she said. "Chill out. Lighten up. I thought we were having fun."

Katiya giggled. "I like her, Quin." She gave Katie a charming smile. "I'm happy to meet you." Then she paused. "Our names are the same, you know? Katie. Katiya. Maybe we be friends."

Katie shook the other woman's hand, touched by the woman's apparent sincerity. "I'd like that. Thanks for your help."

"Enjoy the dress."

"Enjoy the history professor."

Out on the sidewalk, Quin shot her a puzzled look. "What was that all about?"

"After Katiya and Zachary called it quits, she found a history professor and married him. He's her soulmate. Her words. Not mine."

"Soulmate?"

"Some people think it's a real thing."

He pulled her beneath the shade of an awning. "And what about you, Katie Duncan. Are you looking for *your* soulmate?"

Six

Katie sucked in a sharp breath, shocked to her core. She hadn't anticipated such a loaded question in the middle of the street in broad daylight. Weren't men supposed to lead up to this kind of thing?

Quin looked dead serious. His vivid sapphire eyes seemed to burn from within. In about three seconds she was going to melt into a puddle on the sidewalk. And not from the summer heat.

She swallowed hard. "What are you doing?" she asked, trying to breathe. Maybe it was the exhaust fumes from all those yellow cabs making her gulp for oxygen.

He touched her bottom lip with a single finger-tip, barely stroking. "Weighing the odds. Gauging my chances."

"Chances of what?"

His mouth quirked at the corner. "You told me you still wanted me. Did you mean that?"

"I don't know *what* you're talking about."

"Liar…"

The intensity in his gaze made her shiver despite the temperature. "Maybe I was joking," she said. "I'm always sticking my foot in my mouth."

He cupped her face, his thumb caressing her cheekbone. "Don't be afraid, Kat. I can't explain what happened before. In fact, I've racked my brain trying to remember what dumbass thing I did to drive you away."

"It wasn't you," she muttered, suddenly near tears. "It was me."

He frowned. "You're not making sense."

She took a deep breath. This wasn't the time to fall apart. "You and I are *not* soulmates," she said firmly. "I never thought we were. That's the answer to your question. I suppose most women want to believe that their perfect match, their perfect man, is out there somewhere. You're wonderful, Quin, but you and me together…" She trailed off, searching for the exact words to make him understand. "We're *fun*. We're hot in the sack. But we're not soulmates. I walked away two years ago, because I didn't want to have my heart broken."

There. That was about as honest as she could be.

Something flickered in his eyes. Perhaps he hadn't expected her to be so blunt. "I see."

"I shouldn't have said I still wanted you."

"Because it's not true?" Now the set of his jaw was grim.

"Because it would be a mistake, and we're both old enough to learn from our mistakes."

He shook his head slowly. "I'm the guy who plunged down a mountain with a bum knee and almost killed myself. Because I was too stubborn and impatient to wait for the all clear. I'm not known for being levelheaded when it comes to things I want."

"Like skiing?"

"Like you."

His honesty deserved honesty in return. She tilted her face to his. "Then let's make our mistakes, Quin. Kiss me."

He slid his hand behind her neck, pulling her close. When his lips touched hers, she leaned into him with a mortifying whimper of pleasure and shock and delight. Eight million people in the big city, and all Katie could hear was the sound of labored breathing—Quin's and her own.

She had forgotten how good he tasted. A tiny hint of chocolate from the mini éclairs at the fancy salon lingered at the corner of his mouth. She kissed it away. Quin groaned and shuddered. It had always been like this whenever they touched. Raw insanity. Endless need.

"Quin…" She whispered his name, dizzy with wanting him. She had tried to be good and smart and careful with her emotions. But it all came down to this. The laser focus that had made him a champion raked her into his orbit.

He cursed under his breath and backed away. Streams of humanity ebbed and flowed around them. "We should head for the museum," he said gruffly. "If not, we won't make our dinner reservation. I'm sure you want time to shower and relax before we go."

She swallowed, nodding. "That would be nice." She reached out and squeezed his hand. "Truce?"

He nodded, his fingers warm and firm against hers. "Truce." Without asking, he hailed a cab. Katie would have been happy to walk, but Quin was right. If she was to see any of the Met at all and still have time to change, there was no opportunity to dawdle.

When the cabbie dropped them at the curb on Fifth Avenue, Katie stared up at the large flight of steps. "I had no idea the building was so big."

Quin curled an arm around her waist, guiding her among clumps of tourists. "In 1870, when the Met was founded, it owned not a single work of art. Now, some 150 years later, the permanent collection numbers around two million items, only a fraction of which are on display. And that begs the question—where do you want to start?"

Katie grinned, happy despite the simmering tension between them. "Van Gogh, Renoir and the Tiffany glass. That will do for today."

Quin blinked. "I didn't expect you to be quite so *prepared.*"

"I'm a planner. Farrell can tell you that. There's a time and place for spontaneity, but my initial foray into the third most visited museum in the world is an occasion for careful attack."

He kissed her cheek and tucked a stray piece of hair behind her ear. "Your wish is my command."

Quin bought their tickets and grabbed several brochures. After studying the maps to refresh his memory, he nodded. "One level up." He steered her without hesitation to the second-floor gallery that included French Impressionists. When Quin took her hand, her heart turned over in her chest. They saw the Manets and the Monets. The Cézannes and the Cassatts. Van Gogh. Degas. Pissarro.

It was too much. Room after room of art. The color and light and passion that had survived through the centuries and across the miles. She felt overwhelmed. She and Quin turned a corner, and suddenly, she found what she was looking for. "Here it is," she said softly, speaking more to herself than to her companion. Standing in front of the large canvas, she felt her eyes burn.

"Why this one?" Quin asked quietly.

She shot him a watery smile. "When I was eight years old, I desperately wanted to take piano lessons. But my parents were barely getting by. I didn't even get a *maybe* from either one of them. A friend of our family, down the street, owned a piano. She let me peck around sometimes after school, but she didn't really know how to play. The instrument had belonged to her grandmother, so our friend kept it for sentimental reasons. It was scarred and out of tune, but to me it was magical."

"And the Renoir? *Two Young Girls at the Piano*?" He pulled her close.

Katie rested her head on his shoulder, inhaling his familiar scent. Was it possible for a man as wealthy as Quin to understand a child's vulnerability and yearning? Could a man who bought paintings or pianos as easily as a pack of gum recognize a woman's deep need to have dreams?

She sighed. "That same neighbor made a trip to New York one summer. She sent me a postcard of this painting. I still have it."

Quin often stared danger in the face. Every time he stood at the apex of a black diamond slope, his adrenaline surged and his heart raced. He was braced for any and all eventualities.

Today felt oddly the same but terrifyingly different. Spending so much time with Katie in a nonsexual setting these past three weeks had caused him to see her through a different lens. She was a beautiful, sexy woman. That, he had known before. Known it and been terribly disappointed when she walked away for reasons he still didn't quite understand.

Maybe that was the problem. He had been blinded by lust in the past—too hungry for her to see or understand that Katie was a woman of many facets. Because he hadn't known how to get close to her, he'd used his money to woo her.

But what he felt now was not as easily explained as lust. She had become more real and multidimensional to him. Katie was a fascinating, complicated woman.

He wanted her in his life, and he liked making her happy. Could one person even do that for another?

"We should go," he said gruffly. "If you want to see the Tiffany exhibit."

Katie glanced at her watch. "Oh gosh, yes."

Even though she agreed, he sensed her reluctance to leave the Renoir behind.

"We could stop by again tomorrow," he said.

"No." She shook her head as they returned to the main floor. "I knew I would only scratch the surface. I'll come back one day."

After a quick blitz through the incredible stained glass creations of Louis Tiffany, they grabbed a cab and rushed back to the hotel. In the elevator, Katie was subdued, her gaze downcast. He wanted to know what she was thinking. Memories of the kiss they had shared earlier kept him jittery and hungry. Would anything happen tonight?

He could press the issue. Katie wanted him.

But he was ruefully aware that she didn't *want* to want him. The distinction was tough on a man's ego.

In the hallway outside their rooms, he put a finger beneath her chin and locked his gaze with hers. "It's your decision," he said quietly. "But I want you tonight. Think about it. We're good together. Nothing that feels so damn fantastic could be wrong."

She didn't exactly answer him. And he hadn't exactly asked a question. They were each dancing around a conundrum.

Instead, she took her keycard from her purse. "What time do I need to be ready?"

"We're meeting the guys in the theater district at six. But it will be rush hour, so we need to allow forty-five minutes at least."

"So five fifteen?"

"That's about it."

She unlocked her door and bumped it open with one hip. "Today was fun. Thank you for taking me to the museum."

"And the shopping?" He couldn't resist teasing her.

Katie shook her head, her expression wry. "That was mostly for your benefit, I think. But yes, it was enjoyable."

"Lukewarm praise."

"I'll text you when I'm ready."

"I could wash your back," he offered. Even the lighthearted joke made his sex lift and swell.

Katie went up on her toes and kissed his cheek. "Behave yourself, Quinten Stone. Some itches are best left unscratched."

After her pointed dismissal, he sulked in his room for half an hour, and then had to take the quickest shower on record. That and shaving left him little time to wrestle with his tuxedo and bow tie. It was probably too hot to get geared up in this monkey suit, but he wanted to give Katie the whole night-on-the-town experience.

When he was ready, he glanced in the mirror. His customary tan was paler than most summers. The man in the reflection had spent far too much time indoors recently.

Three more weeks of *taking it easy*. The prospect

frustrated the hell out of him. He was in New York. Three airports at his disposal. He could be on a flight to Chamonix or Megeve tomorrow afternoon.

If he was careful, he could fly under the radar when it came to the pro circuit. Try a few green and blue slopes. Test out his new hardware with no one watching.

Two things stopped him. Number one, he had promised Farrell and Zachary that he would follow the doctor's orders this time. And two, he didn't want to give up the next three weeks with Katie.

It was possible he was setting himself up for a second painful rejection. Taking Katie to bed was risky. Especially since he hadn't a clue what went on inside that fascinating brain of hers. But he had to take the chance.

When he knocked on her door a short while later, he shifted from one foot to the other, restless and unsettled. Why the hell had he agreed to meet his brothers for dinner? He should have locked Katie in his hotel room and kept her entertained until morning.

Without warning, the door swung inward, and suddenly he was staring at a vision. A sexy, mouthwatering vision.

"You look amazing," he said hoarsely. He was gobsmacked and trying hard not to show it.

"Thank you." Her smile was almost shy, as if she were on the way to prom and he was her high school date.

Her dress, however, was *not* prom material. It sizzled with sexual innuendo sewn into every thread.

Hell, he was pretty sure Katie was naked underneath that dress Katiya had procured. In addition to being slashed to her navel in front and halfway down her back, the black gown was slit up one leg, tantalizingly high on her slender, toned thigh.

"We could stay in tonight," he said, deadly serious.

"I want to see the musical." Her brown eyes danced with humor. "And have dinner with your family. And enjoy Times Square after dark. Staying home would be boring."

He danced his mouth over hers, half-desperate, but waiting for a signal that she was receptive. "Not the way you and I would do it."

Katie blushed to her hairline and returned the kiss for a good thirty seconds, her lips soft beneath his. She broke free, panting. "I could be persuaded," she said. "But don't, Quin. Please. We're all dressed up, and I want to have fun. *Not* in bed," she said quickly.

"Spoilsport."

He tamped down his hunger and tried to think about something other than the shape of Katie's breasts beneath the silky black fabric. Her beaded nipples were easily visible. What was a man supposed to do? Look the other way? Wear a blindfold?

Oops. Bad choice. Now he was seeing Katie in his bed playing the dominatrix.

More than one male head turned as they made their way through the lobby to the car. The restaurant where they were meeting Farrell and Zachary was on the way to Midtown. It was old and filled with dark colors and leather seating and the heads of long-dead trophy animals high on the walls. Three decades ago, it would also have been filled with cigar smoke. In the twenty-first century, though, the ambience had changed. One of the city's finest chefs reigned over the award-winning kitchen.

Quin focused his gaze on the snarled traffic outside his window and tried not to fixate on the way Katie's cute knee and smooth thigh peeked through the slit in her dress. His throat was dry. His sex was hard as stone, aching. He'd always been a leg man.

A few moments ago, she had taken out a tiny cosmetic bag to repair her lipstick. The quick, feminine movements made him want to kiss her all over again.

What would it take to get her into his bed tonight? He knew Katie wanted him. He would kneel at her feet if he thought it would work. How could either of them resist this gnawing attraction any longer? It was like trying to ignore the tsunami rushing toward the beach.

At last, they pulled up in front of their destination. The doorman rushed to open Katie's side of the car and was rewarded with a sensual, unwittingly teasing dance as she exited. The poor man nearly swallowed his tongue.

Quin slid across the seat and followed her out. He started to take her arm, but touching her right now would be courting disaster. His control was iffy. Instead, he turned to tip the driver and tried not to think about dragging Katie beneath him in a huge soft bed and taking her over and over until morning.

Fortunately for Quin, Farrell and Zachary beat

them to the restaurant. Both men shook Katie's hand, and Farrell even gave her a quick little hug. He and Katie were tight.

The maître d' showed them to their reserved spot. Quin took a seat at Katie's right elbow. Their knees bumped underneath the table. She shot him a look that sent heat straight to his groin. "I'm starving," she said.

Seven

Katie was enjoying herself, and the evening had barely started. Quin's mood was brooding and dangerous. Sexual need hovered just beneath the surface of his debonair exterior.

In his classic tux, he looked every inch the wealthy businessman. She wanted to gobble him up, though that was a clichéd way to describe her need to get naked with him.

His brothers were both impressive male specimens, but Katie couldn't take her eyes off Quin. He exuded confidence and a rakish virility that made her breath catch in her throat.

Was it something as simple as pheromones? She'd been telling the truth when she said he wasn't her soulmate. But Lord help her, he was gorgeous enough to make any woman reckless.

Moments later, Zachary and Quin spotted a mutual acquaintance at the bar. They excused themselves and strode across the crowded restaurant, their shoulders broad and eerily similar.

Farrell leaned forward, his expression harried. "I know I said six weeks, but *please* come back to work Monday. We're drowning without you."

"I'm pretty sure you're not serious," Katie said, laughing. "But your flattery is much appreciated."

"It's not flattery if it's true. You run the R & D department so well, I've always been able to concentrate on design. Now I'm having to put out fires, too. I swear I'm giving you a raise when you get back."

"It's nice to be needed. Job security and all that."

Farrell sat back in his chair, his amusement fading. "How's it going? You can tell me the truth. My brother can be a pain in the ass. Has he been kind to you? Considerate?"

She flashed back to that moment on a hot New York sidewalk earlier today. When she had felt the press of Quin's erection against her abdomen as they kissed. "Yes, of course," she insisted, her face heating. "Everything is going well. We'll be completely caught up when I come back to Portland."

"Any signs of possible espionage?"

"We've come across a few odd glitches in numbers. Nothing definitive. Most of it can be written off as random errors. So far, there's no proof that anything out of the ordinary is going on."

"Good. Maybe we're all being paranoid. And what about my baby brother's mental state? I know he's not chatty about his feelings, physical or otherwise, but I'm hoping he's climbed out of that dark place he wallowed in after the skiing accident. Quin thinks anyone can do anything if they only try hard enough. That's not always true."

"I know. He mentions skiing. Now and again. I'm not a mind reader, though. A man that intense won't give up his dreams lightly."

"My brother is a good guy," Farrell said. "The car accident was a tragedy in more ways than one." He hesitated. "I know Quin can be blunt and stubborn and cantankerous. If you ever find yourself feeling uncomfortable or you simply decide you've had enough, call me and I'll get you out of there, no questions asked."

"Farrell—"

He stopped her. "No, I'm serious. I've felt guilty about you ever since Zachary and I cooked up the plan to make *our* lives easier. We dropped you in the middle of the woods with a man you barely know. You're far away from your friends and your family. I'm sorry about all of it."

"Farrell," she said quietly, glancing over her shoulder to make sure the other two brothers were still occupied.

"Yes?" He leaned forward, perhaps sensing her need for privacy.

"Quin and I dated two years ago. We were lovers," she clarified. No need to dance around the issue.

"Neither of us wanted gossip at work, so we kept the relationship under wraps. It ended abruptly about six months before your father died."

Farrell's eyes widened as a look of discomfort washed over his face. "Oh hell. It's even worse than I thought. We sent you into exile with a man who dumped you? These last three weeks must have been terribly uncomfortable. I'm *so* sorry, Katie. You're a team player for sure, but I never would have asked this of you if I had known. Why didn't you say something?"

"Um, actually, I was the one to break it off, not Quin."

Farrell's jaw dropped. "*You* dumped *him*?"

Katie frowned. "Yes. Is that so hard to believe? I know your brother is irresistible to the female sex, but you can't honestly tell me I'm the first one to walk away."

"I don't know," Farrell said slowly. "You might actually be."

"Oh, come on." Katie stared at him. "Quin's not great with opening up emotionally. I imagine other girlfriends have been frustrated by that."

"Those zeros in his bank account cover a multitude of sins."

She blinked. "Wow. That's a cold, cynical outlook."

Farrell shrugged. "It's true."

"So no one goes out with you and Zachary and Quin for your glowing personalities and sex appeal?"

"Let's just say it's not the first reason."

"Sucks to be you," she said. "Why don't you give it all away and see what happens?"

Farrell chuckled. "We're lonely, not stupid."

Just then, Quin and Zachary returned.

"Please don't tell your brothers what we talked about," Katie whispered urgently.

"What did we miss?" Zach asked, sitting down and flipping his napkin over his lap.

"I want to thank you again for the *Hamilton* tickets," Katie said. "I'm so excited I can hardly stand it, but I really am sorry your girlfriend couldn't go with you tonight."

Zach's quick smile was charming and carried a lot of voltage. "Not to worry. I've already seen the show twice, and the lady…" He paused and shrugged. "No great loss. You and my brother will love it."

The waiter arrived and took their orders. Shortly after, the same older gentleman returned to pour wine and deliver the appetizers. The conversation picked up again. Quin wanted to know about the day's meeting. While the three brothers discussed SRO business, Katie excused herself and went to the ladies' room.

The décor had been preserved as midcentury modern. Katie perched on a stool and repaired her lipstick. Being with the Stone men all at one time was certainly fun. But it kept a woman on her toes.

She stared at herself in the mirror. What did she really want? Quin had booked two rooms at the hotel. He wouldn't insist if she wanted to sleep alone. The conversation with Farrell had only solidified her doubts.

Two years ago, her breakup with Quin had been excruciating, even though it had been her decision. It had taken her months to get over the loss. Nothing she had seen in Quin recently told her he had changed. Was she being a fool?

This was like the time she'd tried to give up sugar, cold turkey. She'd made it an entire six weeks. Then, on a very difficult day when was feeling low, she had eaten a Hershey's bar, and the sugar cravings came rushing back.

Deciding to sleep with Quin would alter her life once again. She knew it deep in her gut. Did she want a brief, exhilarating physical affair if it meant more heartbreak in the near future?

Did she want a relationship with a man who was so besotted with skiing that he almost killed himself? The Quin who was her lover two years ago had been selfish in many ways. Driven. Unable to look beyond the moment. He'd been impulsive and wildly passionate.

Life with that Quin had been exhilarating to a point. But he had never understood her. Or maybe they had never understood each other.

She frowned at her reflection. Though it had taken patience and a few cusswords, she had finally gotten her hair to cooperate in an elegant French twist. With the expensive new dress and the more dramatic makeup, she didn't look out of place in this world.

But she was. *Her* menu at dinner tonight hadn't listed any prices. She'd heard of such a thing, but she'd never actually seen it in person.

This was a climate where money didn't matter. Well, it *mattered*, duh. But not in the way it mattered in Katie's world—where a broken washing machine or a flat tire or an unexpected car repair could send families into a serious downward financial spiral.

That was the world she had grown up in. Those were the people she knew and loved. With her extremely good job at Stone River Outdoors, she had gradually shifted away from her community in one way. She now had a savings account and a 401(k) and fantastic health insurance.

A single bump in the road wouldn't wipe her out. Even so, she understood her family and childhood friends in a way that Quin simply couldn't. If a man had never known hunger or desperation, it would be hard to empathize with those who had. She didn't blame the Stone brothers for being ridiculously wealthy. They were generous employers.

But there was a stark divide between their life experiences and hers.

She wanted Quin to *see* her. To honor her values and opinions. Otherwise, all they had was sex.

When she returned to the dinner table, all three men stood until she was seated. Their innate courtesy was as flawless as it was instinctive. Perhaps their father hadn't been the best parent, but he had raised his sons to be gentlemen. That much was clear.

When her phone dinged quietly, she slipped it from her clutch and read the text, sighing inwardly. Her face must have given her away.

Quin touched her hand. "Problem?"

She didn't really want to elaborate, but all three men were looking at her with varying levels of interest and concern. "My sister is trying to get her own apartment. She's been sleeping on the sofa at a friend's place. She has the rent covered, but she doesn't have any credit. I need to help her with utility deposits and a pet fee."

Quin made a weird sound beneath his breath and frowned. *"Need?"*

She glared at him. "This is none of your business, Quin."

Zachary seemed shocked, perhaps because he was now the only one ignorant of Quin and Katie's former relationship. "We all have to make those decisions at one time or another," he said. "When I turned twenty-five and inherited a large sum of money my grandparents left me, a lot of my old college buddies started crawling out of the woodwork. It's hard to say no."

Katie shook her head. "My sister isn't like that. She doesn't take advantage of me. But I've been luckier in life. I'm able to help, so I do."

Quin's jaw was tight. "I don't think you've been luckier in life. You've worked your ass off. In college you had *three* part-time jobs just to get through. That was your choice. You've worked your way up at SRO. All that is *you*, Katie. Your sister came from the same family."

In the uncomfortable silence that followed Quin's outburst, Farrell stepped into the breach. He gave his brother a warning stare. "That's a lot of information about a woman on such short acquaintance. Maybe we should talk about something else."

Zachary still looked mystified, as if he had missed part of the conversation. He had. Everyone else at the table knew Katie was far more than a temporary assistant during Quin's recovery.

Fortunately, their meals arrived. In the hustle and bustle of making sure everyone was served, the awkward conversation fell by the wayside.

By the time dinner was finished, it was getting late.

"We should head for the theater," Quin said.

As they all stood, Zachary donned his jacket and picked up his credit card receipt. "You two need to keep an eye on the long-range weather outlook. The forecasters are thinking this latest hurricane may make its way up the coast eventually. Be careful."

"I hope they're wrong," Farrell said. "If we get too much damage, it will slow down the building project at my place. I want the new lab to be my sole work site until we figure out what's going on."

When they left the restaurant, the four adults parted ways. Another hired car was waiting for Katie and Quin. She didn't know what to say to him once they were alone. But she knew how she wanted the evening to end. Had their unexpected quarrel ruined the mood?

Suddenly, he reached across the seat and took her hand. "I'm sorry, Katie. I was out of line. What you do in your private life is none of my concern. Will you forgive me?"

He was genuinely sorry. She could see it in his eyes. A cynical person might think he was mending fences in order to coax her into sex tonight. Katie didn't believe that. Quin was not manipulative. Forceful and persuasive, but not manipulative. "I forgive you," she said.

His small smile was sheepish. "I'm not the easiest man to get along with," he confessed. "I wondered why you broke up with me, but it could have been any one of a dozen reasons."

She shifted on the seat. His forthright description of himself demanded equal honesty, but it would serve no useful purpose. "I think we can forget the past, Quin. We're not going back there. I'd prefer to live in the moment. It's safer that way."

"If that's what you want." The slight crease between his eyebrows told her he wasn't pleased with her answer.

The car slid into a momentarily empty space at the curb. The theater was half a block down the street. Quin and the driver exchanged quick words about a later pickup.

As Quin helped Katie out of the car, he explained, perhaps anticipating her question. "It's almost impossible to get a cab when the theaters let out. I don't want to waste any time getting back to the hotel."

It was a loaded statement. Her stomach flipped and her cheeks burned as his hand gripped hers.

Quin laughed. "You look like a scared rabbit. It's your choice, Kat. It always was."

His words stayed with her all through the fabulous musical. Though the story and the rap lyrics and the music were mesmerizing, she was hyperaware of the man at her side. Zachary's seats were box tickets, only eight chairs in the small balcony overlooking the stage. The two beside Quin and Katie were no-shows, so they had the second row to themselves.

As soon as the lights went down, Quin slid his arm around her. His fingers caressed her bare shoulder. He was warm and large and wonderfully *male* at her side. She wanted somehow to preserve this moment, this entire evening, but it was sand slipping though her fingers. A snowflake disappearing in a warm breath.

When the curtain fell for the final time, the enthusiastic crowd clapped and shouted. The sheer talent of the show's creator was awe-inspiring.

Out on the sidewalk, the heat remained, even after dark. Quin pulled her close, protecting her from the jostling crowd. "Coffee? Dessert?" he asked, his expression warm and happy.

"No, thank you," she said. "Let's go home."

It was a slip of the tongue. The Carlyle wasn't their home. But for tonight, it promised privacy and endless possibilities.

The car was waiting for them one street over. At another moment, Katie might have enjoyed riding the subway. That was a big-city rite of passage she had never experienced. But for now, she was content to be whisked away.

The hotel was quiet when they returned. In the elevator, Quin barely spoke. When they reached their floor and stepped out, Katie took his hand. "Give me half an hour," she said. "Then come to my room."

His eyes flared with shock, quickly followed by heat. "You're sure?" The two words were gruff and gravelly.

She slid her hand behind his neck and pulled his head down for a kiss. "Not really. But I won't change my mind, I promise."

Eight

Quin felt like a condemned man faced with a reprieve. After his stupid stunt at dinner, he thought he'd ruined any chance of the two of them winding up together tonight.

His Katie had a kind heart. Either that, or she was as eager to re-create the magic as he was. He stripped off his tux, showered and changed into light knit pants and a T-shirt. Respectable enough for roaming the halls.

His prep took exactly eleven minutes. Which left him nineteen minutes to get antsy. He was second-guessing himself all over the place. Would Katie regret tonight? He didn't want that. Not at all.

But who was he kidding? No way in hell was he walking away from this chance to be with the woman who turned him inside out. He ached for her. In all the months since the accident that derailed his life, sexual needs had taken a back seat to pain and therapy and cumulative weeks in the hospital.

Now his libido had roared to life.

At twenty-nine and a half minutes, he grabbed up his keycard, deliberately left his phone behind and exited his room. The hallway was empty. At this point, he didn't care. He would have walked stark naked through the lobby for the chance to have sex with Katie again.

They'd had plenty of problems during their relationship, but sexual compatibility hadn't been one of them. When they were in bed together, the world stopped. Nothing mattered but the two of them connecting, skin to skin, shivering breath to ragged heartbeat.

He knocked softly at her door. Insanely long seconds passed before she opened it.

When he saw her, his mouth dried and his already semi-erect sex went on high alert. Either Katie had a thing for sexy sleepwear, or she had come prepared for this weekend with him. He hoped like hell it was the second.

She had showered as he had. Earlier tonight, her elegant hairstyle had bared her neck—sexy in a different way. Now, her silky blond hair, still damp in places, brushed her shoulders.

"You are so damn hot," he muttered. Her mostly sheer black nightgown did little to conceal her budded nipples or anything farther south. He ran a hand down her arm. "I want you, Kat. I know I should be cool about this, but I have to be honest. I haven't been with a woman since the accident. I may disappoint you this first time."

Eyes wide, she took his hand and pulled him inside, closing the door with a gentle shove. "I won't be disappointed, I swear."

He sifted his fingers through her hair, steadied her head in his hands and found her mouth with unerring desperation. "I've missed this," he groaned.

His instinct was to take what he wanted, what they both wanted. But second chances were delicate and prone to collapse. Katie needed more from him than selfish lust. He saw that now. In hindsight, he could identify all the ways he had failed her. This time would be different.

He wasn't the same man.

Her lips were soft and eager. She leaned into him, signaling her readiness. With one arm, he dragged her close, molding their bodies from chest to knee. He could feel every inch of her warm, soft skin.

He was embarrassingly out of control. "I wanted to do this right," he panted.

Katie's laugh was low and knowing. The sound scraped his nerve endings and made the hunger worse. She nipped the shell of his ear with sharp teeth. "I believe you. Let's see what you've got, big guy."

He tugged her wrist, dragging her toward the lavish hotel bed, pausing only to throw back the covers and pillows and bolsters. He shoved them aside and laid Katie in the exact center of the bed. Her hair fanned out in a messy arc over the pillow. Her cheeks were flushed, her gaze soft.

With clenched fists, he forced himself to appreciate the picture she made. His chest heaved. He tried to control his driving need. He wasn't an animal. Still, something primitive stirred within him. Something possessive and determined and demanding.

The sleep pants that rode low on his hips had a single pocket. He had stuffed it with several condoms. Tossing the protection on the bedside table, he lifted his arms and ripped his T-shirt over his head. The stunned way she watched him was gratifying.

He hadn't planned a strip show. But when he dragged his pants down his legs and kicked them aside, Katie's eyes rounded.

Quin took his aching flesh in one hand and fisted it, barely able to touch himself. "Is this what you want, Kat?" The skin was tight, almost painful.

"No." Her brown eyes heated. "I want more. I want it all."

Her words were like a physical blow. He flinched away from them, even as her bold pronouncement ratcheted his hunger upward. His breath sawed in and out of his lungs like a dying man's.

What more could he give her? He had laid his hunger and his fortune at her feet once before, and it hadn't been enough. What else was there?

Ignoring the nuances of her disturbingly ambiguous declaration, he joined her on the mattress. It barely dipped beneath his weight. A bed at the Carlyle wasn't a bad place to restart a sexual relationship that had lain dormant for two years.

He stroked her breast through her nightgown, pinching lightly. The curved mound fit his palm perfectly.

Katie's strangled moan urged him on. Her eyelids fluttered shut. He thought she was going to say something, but if her throat was as tight as his, the ability to speak had eroded rapidly.

Moving his hand to the other breast, he rested his head on her shoulder. She was warm, so warm. Her fingers sifted through his hair, massaging his scalp. This time he twisted the nipple with a firm grip. The raspberry nub was hard now. Puckered. Taut.

He couldn't resist. Shifting positions slightly, he bit down on her tender flesh, just enough to let her know he meant business. Katie's keening moan made the hair on the back of his neck stand up.

When she turned her cheek into his chest, his heart clenched. The gesture of trust affected him more strongly than he would ever admit. He knew that he had failed her somehow in the past. Hurt her.

Whatever it was that had dragged them apart didn't have to happen this time. He could fix it.

The bottom of Katie's gown had twisted around her legs. He tugged it loose and gathered it to her waist. Now his view was unimpeded. Her pink, moist sex was a thing of beauty. Katie was clean-shaven between her legs, but a tiny, heart-shaped fluff of pale hair covered her mons.

He started to shake as if fevered. His need for her scrambled his brain. When he stroked her center,

Katie shook her head wildly. "I'm ready," she said, the words demanding. He might have smiled if he hadn't been out of his mind with lust.

Instead, he grabbed a condom, ripped it open and rolled it carefully over his aching erection. "Katie..." He wanted to say something tender and romantic. Words failed him.

She held out her arms, her eyes heavy-lidded. "I want you, Quin."

Straightforward. Impossible to misinterpret.

He spread her thighs and mounted her, sliding deep with one steady push. Katie whimpered. Her sex clenched around his, eager, ready.

The need to come was almost impossible to hold at bay. Embarrassingly so. In his head, he tried to list the slope gradients of his five favorite ski runs. It didn't work. He ground his pelvis against hers. Was she even close? They had barely started.

Again, he rubbed the base of his sex where it would make the most difference, trying to hit just the right spot.

Katie grabbed his shoulders, her fingernails scoring his hot skin. "I'm so close. Harder, Quin," she begged.

The desperation in her pleas galvanized him. He withdrew almost completely and slammed his body into hers. The connection was messy and raw and inelegant. Any finesse he had once possessed was gone.

All he could see was her beautiful face. All he could feel was a rush of pleasure so intense, it burned to the point of pain.

Katie cried out and wrapped her legs around his waist, lifting into him and taking all he had to give. His own orgasm snapped like the sharp flick of a broken rubber band. He caught his breath and muffled his shout in her shoulder. His world ground to a halt.

It had never been like this. In the past, they had dented his bedroom wall a time or two with the headboard. One night they even broke Katie's bed. It was one of his fondest memories.

But the sex was different now.

Was it the two years of being apart, or had they each changed?

He rolled away from her, trying not to let her see how strung out he felt. His eyes stung.

Without thinking it through, he linked her fingers with his. Her touch was a lifeline in his spinning universe. "Katie?"

"Hmmm?"

"Did you see other men after we broke up?"

It wasn't a fair question. It wasn't his business. But the possessive need to stake a claim made him oblivious to the land mine he had planted.

"Yes."

His heart slugged once in his chest, as if someone had whacked him in the ribs with a baseball bat and cracked bone. Of course she had. The men in Portland weren't blind.

She raised up on one elbow, staring at him, her expression curiously blank. "Did you sleep with other women?"

He closed his eyes, not wanting her to see the truth. "At first. Several of them, actually. I was angry."

"About what?"

He sat up and raked his hands through his hair. "I was angry that you didn't give me a chance to undo whatever stupid thing I had done to make you walk out on us."

All the color drained from her face. Her expression was bleak, tormented. "It wasn't that simple, Quin."

"Nothing ever is…"

"We're better off being friends. Trust me."

"I think you're wrong."

She left him and went to the bathroom. When she returned, she had donned one of the plush hotel robes. Her jaw stuck out at a familiar angle. "I won't re-hash the past, Quin." Her eyes were dark with misery. "We don't have a future. If you want this…" She waved a hand at the bed. "I'll be with you for three more weeks."

Fury flared in his gut. "So take it or leave it?"

She nodded slowly, her lips pressed tightly together. "Yes."

"Okay, then." He shut his mind to the *feelings* that bombarded him. He was a man who didn't trust feelings. Hell, he couldn't even trust his own body anymore. "In that case, come back to bed. I'm not through with you."

He must think I'm a bitch.

Katie's stomach curled. For the briefest of moments, she flashed back to that terrible day with

Quin's father. He had made her feel she was less than nothing. If she'd had any inkling that Quin wanted more than sex, she might have fought for the chance to find out.

His father's cold, dispassionate summation of the truth had shattered her confidence and underscored every one of her doubts about her relationship with Quin.

Even back then, she had realized that Quin could *never* know what had happened. Now that his father was gone, the truth was even more dangerous. Quin had suffered so much. She couldn't add to his pain. But she also couldn't expect anything different from a relationship this time around. Not with the secret she carried.

She stared at her lover, his insolent smile chipping away at the happiness she had experienced only a few minutes ago. Even so, she couldn't look away. Sprawled in her bed, he was the epitome of erotic excess. Sin incarnate. The man with the tender grin and gentle touch had been replaced by a hard-edged billionaire bad boy.

This was the image she had run from two years ago. The hints of darkness inside him had both attracted and repelled her.

The Quin who made love to her tonight was a shock. In a good way. He had been passionate and demanding, though at the same time, protective. Warm. Affectionate.

In trying to guard herself, her words and actions had wrought a terrible change in him. He had withdrawn to a place that suited his lone-wolf personality—a place where he could be in control.

She shed the robe and approached the bed. Quin's unpleasant sneer faded. He blinked as a dark flush of red rode high on his cheekbones. "God, you're gorgeous, Katie Duncan." He reached for her without warning, grabbing her wrist and tumbling her onto the bed.

When she was breathless and pinned beneath his weight, his mood softened. "Hell," he muttered. "I can't stay mad at you. Women have always been a mystery to me. What they want. What they don't want."

"It's not so terribly complicated," she whispered. When she cupped his cheek, his skin was stubbly and warm. "All I want is for you to make love to me over and over again."

The planes of his face grew taut. His eyes glittered. "Lucky for both of us, we're finally on the same page."

She had expected harshness after their conflict. Instead, he gave her aching tenderness. It was like he was two different men. Carefully, he lifted her astride him, but didn't join their bodies. When her hair swung loose and shielded her face, he wound handfuls of it around his fingers and pulled her head down, so he could kiss her.

Her breasts pillowed against his hard chest. The contrast between their bodies, male and female, was both arousing and astonishing. How could two people so different in every way be so perfectly attuned in bed?

He smelled amazing. Warm male skin and the hotel's shower gel. It was a heady combination. She nipped his chin with her teeth. "How many condoms did you bring?" she asked, the question breathless.

"Not nearly enough." He sighed audibly, amusingly crestfallen. The kiss deepened. He slid his tongue between her lips, tasting, seducing.

Her bones turned to water. She wanted to climb inside his skin and occupy the same space, breathe the same air. Behind her, his considerable erection bumped her bottom. "You seem to have a problem, Mr. Stone. May I help you with that?"

He was panting now, his fingers bruising her skin where he clenched her ass. "Can't. Reach. Condoms."

"Hang on, Quin. I'll do it." Easier said than done. He was holding her so tightly, there wasn't much room to maneuver. When she bumped her elbow on the corner of the small bedside table, pain shot up her arm. Still, she persevered. At last, the small packet was in reach.

She held it up in triumph. "Got it!"

This reunion was still new enough that she didn't feel comfortable performing such an intimate task. Quin must have sensed her unease. He set her aside for a moment, dealt with the necessary protection and then rolled onto his hip to face her.

She felt the hot color that stained her cheeks.

Quin chuckled. "I can't believe you still blush."

"Not all of us are as world-weary as you are, Quin

Stone." She sniffed. "And not all of us have a hundred notches on our belt."

One masculine eyebrow went up. He traced her nose with a delicate touch. "You're not wearing a belt, Kat. And for the record, your impressions of me are way off base. I told you I haven't been with a woman since the accident."

"But that's—"

He put a hand over her mouth, silencing her startled reaction. "I really don't want to waste this condom. Can we talk about this later? At a less *critical* juncture?"

She glanced down at his erection. Despite the momentary pause in the action, Quin was still locked and loaded. "My apologies. Carry on."

"So it's all up to me?" He rolled onto his back and slung one arm across his forehead. "Maybe I want you to take the lead."

She was skeptical. "Then maybe we put the condom on too soon," she said tartly.

"You're a creative woman. Oral sex isn't the only thing men like. Surprise me."

"But won't your…" She waved her hand in the general direction of his straining, swollen sex.

His grin was tight. "If you're concerned that I might *deflate* before I get inside you, don't be. The way I feel right now, I might be hard till Labor Day."

Nine

Quin loved teasing Katie. She rose to the bait so beautifully.

Her eyes rounded. "Labor Day? That's a weird holiday to pick."

He took her hand and put it on his chest. "Please, Kat. I can't wait much longer."

It was true. His sex throbbed like a damned toothache. When she caressed his taut belly, his skin broke out in gooseflesh. This was a gamble on his part. Perhaps he had never let Katie feel the power she had over him.

"Do whatever you want," he croaked. "I'm all yours."

It was true he regretted donning the protection too soon. He'd been intent on penetration at all costs. At the last minute, he had backed off. Getting Katie to trust him meant letting her take the wheel now and then.

Her expression was endearingly intense. Her light caresses were almost as arousing as if she had taken him in her mouth. They would get to that. He hoped. For now, though, he was her willing subject.

Katie touched every part of his body. Almost. When she bent and kissed the arches of his feet, he almost came off the bed.

"Too much?" she asked, her expression guileless. Big brown eyes dared him to complain.

He shrugged. "You startled me. That's all. I'm ticklish."

"Ah." She worked her way back up his body. Shins. Knees. Thighs. Mostly kissing. Sometimes biting. His fingers clenched in the sheets. Sweat beaded his brow. Her scent filled his lungs.

When she bypassed the part of him that needed her most, he wanted to cry and curse. She had taken his challenge and run with it. Even if it killed him, he was determined not to crack.

She stroked his rib cage with two hands. Then she cupped his face between her palms and kissed him deeply. It was *her* tongue in *his* mouth this time. He would never have described Katie as a passive lover in the past. But unwittingly, he had unleashed a wild, sensual temptress tonight.

He couldn't decide which was worse. Eyes open, or eyes closed. He was breathing so fast the risk of hyperventilation was real.

"Katie," he said. The single word was all he could manage.

"Yes?"

He gulped air. "Enough, Kat. Please."

She had been leaning over him, her body pressed to his chest. Now she straightened and lifted up onto her knees. "I knew I could make you cry uncle," she said teasingly. But there was no smug triumph in her words. Her gaze was soft and affectionate.

He was enjoying himself. What red-blooded heterosexual man wouldn't? But some hazy discontent niggled at his composure. Something about the earlier conversation. Three weeks. Convenient. Temporary.

Maybe there was more. Maybe he *wanted* more.

He had lost his father and almost lost the use of his leg. He'd had to give up competitive skiing with no real possibility that he might ski again at all, thanks to his reckless behavior. Couldn't the Fates be kind? Couldn't Katie be his consolation prize? The one perfect, happy part of a screwed-up life?

She scooted backward and carefully lowered herself onto his erection. The slick friction and tight squeeze of her body on his was nirvana. Only the fact that he had come so recently allowed him to fully enjoy this next act. Watching Katie was almost as exhilarating as being inside her.

He deliberately maintained his passive role. When she hesitated, he urged her on. "Take what you want, Kat. Give us what we both need."

Her languid movements accelerated. She rode him well, though her technique was endearingly unpracticed. He lifted into her, thrusting upward to meet her descent. Suddenly, he was consumed with the need to know if she had done this exact ballet with another man.

An earthquake of fire burned jagged fault lines through his body without warning. He'd thought he had things under control. Apparently not.

"Sorry," he groaned, rolling her beneath him. He lost it. Completely.

The room disappeared. He locked eyes with the woman beneath him. "I don't want it to end, Kat." He meant the current frenzy, but he could have been talking about the big picture. Blindly, he drove into her. In some dim corner of his brain, he heard the echoes of Katie's climax.

He went deeper. Harder. He felt invincible. As if he were standing at the top of a mountain he'd wanted to scale for far too long. And then it happened, that intense, shattering moment of joy when he slipped over the edge and let himself fall.

Katie wrapped her arms around him. "Yes, Quin. Yes…"

After that, silence reigned but for the beating of his heart in his ears and the ragged unison of their breathing.

It might have been minutes or hours before he was himself again. He honestly couldn't say.

Katie had reached out at one point and awkwardly pulled the covers to their shoulders. The AC was highly efficient. Neither of them had thought to adjust it before now. Cool air bathed their damp bodies in currents of icy chill, drying the sweat on their skin. The quiet hum of the unit masked any noises outside.

With the drapes still open, the lights of the city shone red and gold and green and white and every color in between. Most people were home by now, but he knew the streets in some parts of town still teemed with activity on a Friday night. Around the Carlyle, the neighborhood was quiet.

At last, when he could function, he lifted himself off Katie and stumbled into the bathroom. When he returned, he found her sound asleep. As he stood in the doorway watching her, his heart clenched in his chest. She was right. By every metric, they were an unlikely couple.

He shut off the unpleasant thought, determined to live in the moment.

Katie was his for now. That would have to do.

When Katie woke up in the middle of the night needing to pee, she glanced at her phone. It was 5:00 a.m. Quin had made love to her again somewhere around two thirty. Now he slept like the dead, one heavy arm slung over her waist as if trying to keep her prisoner.

Drowsy and sated, she lingered in bed, not wanting to give up such perfection. Outside the window, lights from tall buildings created a warm, comforting glow. If New York was the city that never slept, a person could feel safe knowing that somebody somewhere was keeping watch.

At last, she eased free of Quin's unconscious

embrace and padded to the bathroom. Her muscles were stiff, and her sex was puffy and sore. When she pressed a cold washcloth between her legs, she sighed.

This was the memory she had tried so hard to suppress. *This* smugly happy feeling of repletion. She hadn't been a virgin when she and Quin first hooked up. But her few relationships hadn't prepared her for the hurricane that was sex with Quin. He was rough and wild and intensely arousing.

He never did anything to hurt her. He was endlessly tender. But that same tenderness was wrapped in masculine determination, carrying her to a place of physical bliss so deep and so wide, she nearly lost herself.

Sometimes she wondered if she broke up with him not because of the money squabbles, but because the feelings he invoked terrified her. She didn't want to always be teetering on the edge of insanity. It was a dangerous place to live.

When she slipped back into bed, the breath from his disgruntled muttering warmed her chilled skin. He wrapped two big muscular arms around her and pulled her close. The man's body radiated heat like a furnace. She burrowed into his side and soothed herself by listening to the steady, rhythmic beat of his heart.

He was so *alive*, so willing to tempt fate on the slopes, to live life on his terms.

As she drifted off to sleep, she prayed that she would have the strength to leave when it was time to go.

* * *

When she woke again, it was morning. Clouds had rolled in. Though the day was gray, nothing could dent her euphoria. She rolled over to see if Quin was awake. Her heart stopped when she saw a pillow with only the indentation of his head. The sheets were cold.

Then she saw the tiny white note. He'd torn off half a sheet from the hotel notepad.

Katie—
Gone for coffee, condoms and croissants. Back soon...

Quin

Her smile grew. With no idea when her lover would return, she dashed into the bathroom and bundled her hair into a towel. Then she grabbed a quick shower to freshen up for whatever might come next.

She had just finished getting dressed and was gathering her hair into a ponytail when the door to the corridor opened without warning. Quin burst into the room, bringing with him the irresistible aroma of hot coffee and freshly baked pastries.

He tossed the smallest of the white paper bags on the dresser. Waving two large cups, he grinned at her. "Breakfast is served, madam."

She cocked her head and returned the smile. "You do know we're staying at the Carlyle? I'm fairly certain room service would have delivered anything and everything we wanted."

"Not condoms," he said, smirking. "Besides, I needed a walk. And I happened to remember a great little patisserie a few blocks over on Third Avenue. The real deal. Almost like being in Paris. You hungry?" He waved the bag in front of her face.

The scent of breakfast made her stomach flip. "Oh yeah."

Before she could claim her share, a discreet knock sounded at the door. Quin checked the peephole. "Ah. Reinforcements."

Apparently, as he had entered the hotel, he had paused to order fresh-squeezed orange juice, perfect strawberries and two extra pots of coffee. Along with a serving trolley draped in white linen and laden with heavy silverware and a single rose in a crystal vase.

Wow.

Quin tipped the uniformed hotel employee and shut the door. He pulled two small chairs to flank the table. "C'mon. I'm starving. I expended a lot of calories last night."

Her face heated. "On my way."

When Quin held out her chair, he bent to kiss the side of her neck just below her ear. The tantalizing caress sent shivers down her spine. He was so relaxed, so natural.

She felt vulnerable and unsure. How did a woman and a man follow a night like last night?

Apparently, Quin believed the answer was food. He ripped open the large paper bag and waved his hand, wafting the smell in her direction. "Croissants. Baked this morning. Chocolate-filled. Plain, with plenty of butter and orange marmalade. And my personal favorite—a lemon, raspberry and ricotta combo. We can cut them in half if you want to try them all."

Katie's stomach rumbled audibly. She tore off a piece of the chocolate-filled croissant and stuffed it in her mouth. "Oh. My. Gosh." The flavors exploded on her tongue. Like Mrs. Peterson's crème brûlée, almost better than sex. *Ha!* Not even close.

Quin poured their coffee, preparing Katie's the way she liked it without asking. Did it mean anything if a man remembered one sugar, no cream after two years apart? Maybe not. In recent weeks she'd been drinking English breakfast tea at his house in Maine. So the memory was an old one.

She took a sip of coffee. The fabulous elixir was still surprisingly hot enough to make her tongue tingle. "How often are you in Paris?"

He had to chew and swallow before he could answer. "Three or four times a year. Stone River Outdoors owns a flat in Montmartre. We do a lot of business in Europe, so Paris is a great hub for us."

A flat in Montmartre? Good grief. He said it offhand, the same way she might refer to a Taco Bell in Portland. Again, her doubts surfaced. Of course, if all of this was only temporary, why was she worried at all?

They devoured the half dozen croissants in short order, Quin's four to her two. He reached across the table and caressed her chin. "Marmalade," he said soberly. But his eyes danced.

She grabbed his hand and held it to her cheek. "What's in the other bag, Quin?"

He shrugged. "Possibilities. For later. Right now, we're going to play tourist. That's why I brought you to New York."

She shook her head slowly. "No. The museums can wait. I want *you* for breakfast."

His eyes flared, those extraordinary irises sparking with heat. "Are you sure, Kat? This weekend is my gift to you."

"I thought this trip was about *your* cabin fever."

He shrugged, sheepish at being caught out in a lie. "I wanted to get away. That much is true. But when Zachary offered us the Broadway tickets, I thought it would make you happy. I like making Katie Duncan happy."

Those last six words were uttered with such raw sincerity it would be hard to fake. "This room is expensive," she said. "I think we should get our money's worth. You know how I like to be thrifty."

"I do know," he said wryly.

"Then come to bed with me. All that coffee has me hyped up. I need to work off some energy."

As it turned out, they didn't leave the suite until dinnertime. Quin was insatiable. So was she. If living in a fantasy was wrong, then her punishment would come later. For now, she was committed to enjoying the moment, a moment that was impossibly wonderful.

The sex ranged from playful to hungry to slow and sweet. In between, they napped, wrapped in each other's arms. She had thought she knew Quin. But he showed her new sides to him that their earlier affair had never revealed. It was as if he had dropped some unseen armor.

Katie's emotions were full. Happiness and peace. Fear and trembling. She was going to fall long and hard.

As she rested her cheek over Quin's heart, she knew the consequences would be worth every minute she spent in this bed.

Finally, he rolled over and yawned and glanced at the clock. "Good Lord, Kat. We're gonna need a redo of this weekend."

She lifted an eyebrow? "The sex? Count me in. But if you're talking about all the rest, I've seen plenty of movies set in New York. I swear I can fill in the blanks. Besides, you took me to see *Hamilton*. That was a great start. I'll save the Empire State Building for another day."

He yawned again. "Sorry," he muttered. He picked up his phone. "I know a couple of great restaurants you'd like. Let me see where I can get a reservation. I may have left it too late."

She snatched his phone and tossed it on the far side of the huge bed. "I still haven't gotten my hot dog from a street vendor. Couldn't we find one and have a picnic in Central Park?"

"Half the benches have pigeon poop on them, and the park will be full of joggers and tourists."

She pinched his cheek. "*I'm* a tourist, remember?

You said you wanted to make me happy." She batted her lashes dramatically.

"Unbelievable." He rolled his eyes, laughing. "We're surrounded by some of the finest haute cuisine in the world, and you want a meat stick of unknown origin?"

"Geez, Quin. Do you rich guys ever get down and dirty with the masses? Live a little. There's a good chance we *won't* get food poisoning."

"I wouldn't take bets on that," he grumbled. "But if I'm going to die later, I think I need a reason to live right now."

He pretended to roll on top of her. She shoved at his chest, knowing that for once, he was kidding about sex. "We skipped lunch, you maniac. You have to feed me. I'm pretty sure I read that in the fine print somewhere."

"You are such a diva," he complained. "First you want breakfast, then lunch. Now a hot dog? The things I do for you…"

She sat up, clutching the sheet to her chest. "I never *got* lunch," she reminded him. "Give me five minutes in the bathroom to get dressed. Then it's your turn."

"We could shower together," he said, looking hopeful.

"Put a pin in that. I could be persuaded. But not until I've had my hot dog."

Ten

Quin helped Katie into the cab and slid in beside her. He was relaxed and mellow, definitely inclined to indulge the woman sitting near him. She had begged to walk to the corner and hail a cab the old-fashioned way, insisting that summoning a private car via phone was no fun at all.

Now he leaned forward to speak to the cabbie, feeling a bit ridiculous. "The lady wants to find a street vendor and buy a hot dog. I'm willing to double the fare. Can you help us out with that? But not too far, because we're taking it to the park afterward."

The cabbie nodded, though his dubious expression in the rearview mirror was a dead giveaway. Quin presumed the poor man probably dealt with crazy tourists on a regular basis. This impromptu hot dog trip might be the most boring part of his day.

Fortunately, they found what Katie wanted without driving across town. Maybe the driver had a relative in the food services industry. Whatever the explanation, soon the cab was idling at the curb while Katie and Quin bought bottled water and hot dogs with all the trimmings.

When they were back in the car, the cabbie swung around the block and headed toward the park. "Does it matter where I drop you?" he asked.

"Nope. Anywhere will do," Quin said.

Katie held the large bag in two arms. Quin had insisted on multiple hot dogs, bags of chips and some packaged oatmeal cookies. His companion stared into the bag lustfully, pausing to inhale now and then.

The cab rolled to a halt at a popular entrance not far from the hotel. The unadorned path led down a slope into the heart of the park. Quin paid the driver. "This way," he said to Katie. They found an unoccupied bench and put the food between them. "Happy now?" he asked, smiling. The humidity was down. Though the park was indeed crowded, the summer evening felt near perfect.

"Definitely." She handed him one of the all-the-way dogs. She had added only mustard and pickles to hers. She took a big bite and sighed.

"What's wrong?" he asked.

"Nothing. Not really. It's just not quite as good as the ones you get at a baseball stadium."

"I don't want to say I told you so."

"But you're gonna..."

He tucked her hair behind her ear. "Maybe."

"Well, I don't care. Even if the hot dog isn't the icon of culinary enjoyment I had hoped, the setting more than makes up for it. I had no idea Central Park was so big."

"It's two and a half miles long and half a mile wide."

"I'm impressed." She licked mustard off her fingers one at a time, which shouldn't have been particularly erotic to Quin, but it was. "Are we going to walk after this?"

"I thought we would. If you still want to."

"I'm game." Her neat khaki shorts bared legs that were slim and strong and capable. Her running shoes were turquoise and matched her nylon, scoop-necked top.

They finished everything but the cookies. Quin looked at the cellophane-wrapped sweets. The expiration date was eight months in the future. "Let's order dessert from room service when we get back," he said. "The hotel restaurant has a great pastry chef. Triple chocolate cake, bourbon pecan pie, gourmet banana pudding slathered with whipped cream. You name it." He dropped the two unopened packages in the trash.

Katie tried to stop him at the last second, but she was too late. The additive-laden snacks were down in the hole with melting ice cream, empty drink cans and already-chewed gum.

"Why did you toss them?" she cried. "That's so wasteful."

"It was a couple of bucks, Katie. No big deal."

"I could have given them to a street person."

Suddenly, there was tension back in the equation. And it wasn't the sizzling, nerve tingling kind. "I'm sorry," he said stiffly. "I'll ask next time. Let's go."

He walked swiftly, stretching his leg and his knee until the muscles burned. The doctor had said to take it easy for six more weeks. Didn't get much easier than a stroll through the park.

Katie walked beside him except for the moments when people passed them. Quin showed her the *Imagine* memorial to John Lennon, who had lived nearby and whose ashes had been scattered in the park almost four decades before.

Katie loved the Alice in Wonderland statue, the group of bears sculpture and also the small man-made lake, where adults and children sailed toy boats and made memories.

By the time they hit the pond, they had been walking rapidly for almost an hour. Katie plopped down on a concrete step, pressing the back of her hand to her forehead. "Let's take a break. This is a beautiful spot."

"One of my favorites," he said, sitting hip to hip with his charming but unpredictable companion. He almost curled his arm around her, but Katie had put up some kind of do-not-disturb thing between them. He didn't want to disrupt the momentary accord.

After a few moments, she shot him a sideways glance. "Why doesn't Stone River Outdoors have offices here?" she asked.

"Manhattan real estate is too damn expensive. Plus, it's not really necessary. We're so close time-wise. We can easily fly down from Maine and back in a day trip…like Farrell and Zachary did yesterday."

"Ah."

"May I ask you another question?" she said softly, staring out across the water. "It's personal."

His stomach tightened. "Of course."

"I saw your knee—while we were having sex. I'm assuming the two longest, newest scars are from the recent knee replacement."

His hands fisted on his thighs. "Yes."

"I didn't know there were so many others. Scars, I mean."

He shrugged. "They worked hard to rebuild my knee after it was mangled in the car crash."

She touched his leg. "I'm so sorry that happened to you."

His stomach curled. He didn't like talking about the accident. "You said you had a question?"

"Will you be able to ski again competitively?"

He knew the answer, knew it well. But he could barely speak the words. "No. Not a chance," he said bluntly. "Even if I manage to get back out there on the slopes, I won't be able to ski aggressively enough to be a contender. When you're competing in the down-hill events, you have to take chances. You have to snap those quick turns with precision, dig in your skis, gain every possible second. I can't do that any-more."

Admitting the truth to himself *and* to Katie was both cathartic and deeply painful.

She patted his leg, stroking it almost absentmindedly. "And skiing for pleasure?"

"The doc says yes. As long as I don't try too soon and screw things up like I did a few months ago. He thinks when everything heals properly, I should be able to do a nice downhill run on the bunny slopes."

"Seriously?" Her expression was aghast.

"No, not seriously. But it might as well be the bunny slopes. Nothing is going to be the same."

"You could find your joy in other places," she said. The sympathy in her dark eyes was a gift he wasn't willing to accept.

"Skiing is all I have, Katie. The sport has defined me for so long I don't know who I am without the wind and the mountain and the cold sting of snow in my face."

"A lot of wealthy people support charitable causes. They can even change the world. Maybe it's hard to see right now, because you've had so many disappointments. But helping people might be a way you can re-create the fulfillment skiing gave you."

He felt as if she was picking at a scab deep in his soul. "Let's change the subject," he said gruffly. Her slight flinch told him she recognized the *butt-out* subtext. To her credit, she didn't push.

"Okay," Katie said. "Then tell me about Farrell's wife. I've heard snippets of gossip, but I'd like to know the truth. From you."

It was a definite relief to shift the focus away from

the personal topics Quin hadn't even sorted out for himself yet. "Farrell married his high school sweetheart, but only after a long, horrible battle with our father."

"What do you mean?"

He rubbed three fingers in the center of his forehead. "I don't remember if you ever ran into my father at the office. Not likely. He didn't enjoy mingling with the *common* people." Quin snorted. "He didn't much like people at all. To be honest, he spent most of our lives warning us about the *leeches*—his words, not mine—who would try to use us."

Katie shuddered visibly. "What made him like that?"

"Our mother died when I was born. Apparently, a lot of women wanted to help the rich widower grieve. For a price. I think he really loved our mother. I don't know if he was always cynical and hard, but he surely was after she was gone."

"What does that have to do with Farrell?"

"Farrell and Sasha started dating when they were sixteen. Dad didn't like it, but he figured it was puppy love, so he mostly left them alone. Then somehow, Farrell graduated one day and bought Sasha a ring the next."

"Oh dear."

"Yeah. It was romantic as hell, but the old man was furious. He sent Farrell off to college on the West coast and, on the sly, told Sasha that she was ruining Farrell's life. I was still too young to pay much attention to what was going on, but Farrell has told me the stories. Farrell knew that what he and Sasha had was the real deal. But he didn't know what Dad had done to Sasha. Eventually he dragged the truth out of her. It killed him that she had been hurt so badly, especially by *our father.*"

Katie trembled inside. "But you all still had relationships with your father. Was it only because of the business?"

Quin shook his head slowly. "It's a long story, more than you want to hear."

"Okay. Then finish the other one."

"Farrell and Sasha kept in touch by email and phone calls after he went off to college. Then when they both turned twenty-one, Farrell came home, told our father to go to hell and married his sweetheart."

Katie was spellbound. "That's such a beautiful story, at least Farrell's part."

"Not so much after Sasha got sick. Aggressive breast cancer. He lost her when they were both only twenty-five years old."

A single tear rolled down Katie's cheek. Quin caught it with the tip of his finger. "I didn't mean to make you sad."

"I know. I've worked for your brother a long time. I suppose I've always been curious. He never dates anybody that I can tell. Now I know why. I can't imagine losing the love of your life at such a young age. It must have been devastating."

"The tragedy affected all of us. I'd like to believe even the old man felt a shred of guilt, but I don't know. Zachary took the exact opposite road. He's had more females in his life than a cat has kittens. He keeps all his women at arm's length. Calls the shots. Walks away when the relationship reaches its expiration date. He's funny and smart and charming as hell, but he never lets anybody get too close."

"And you, Quin? How did Sasha's death affect you?"

Katie jumped to her feet, jolted by the expression on Quin's face. She wanted to know everything about his past, but not if it meant hurting him. He'd never offered her that kind of personal deep dive before.

"Forget I asked," she begged. "That's way too personal a question between you and me. Sex, yes. Unburdening soul-deep secrets, no."

In her defense, hearing that Mr. Stone Sr. had treated another woman as abysmally as he treated Katie rattled her. She had clung to her desperate humiliation and her injured pride for far too long. The man was dead. He couldn't hurt her anymore. The only person who could mess things up now was Katie herself.

Was she holding Quin to some impossible standard of perfection? God knows, she had plenty of faults of her own. She liked playing the role of savior. She could be too pushy at times. And she had a chip on her shoulder about Quin's money.

Still, her fear held her back, because she wanted him to connect with her intimately. And she wasn't sure such a thing was possible. Even if Quin wanted more than a few weeks of sexual excess, she was scared to think about what that might mean. It was easier and safer to micromanage other people's problems than to take a good, hard look at her own.

She held out her hand, smiling, pretending that she and Quin were nothing more than friends with benefits. "You ready to head back to the hotel? I see a shower in my future."

"*Our* future," Quin said waggling his eyebrows. "Remember?" He rolled to his feet. "I'll wash those spots you can't reach."

She knew he was teasing. Playing the goofball for her amusement. But the words gave her a thrill. Deep in the base of her abdomen, little firecrackers began to ignite.

"Can you run?" she asked.

He stared at her blankly, a crease between his eyebrows. "What do you mean?"

"The doctor. Your recovery. Taking it easy. Can you run?"

He stared at her intently. Suddenly, the wanting and the waiting were back and all mixed up with the emotional wringer he had put her through in telling his family's story.

Quin nodded slowly. "As long as it's not too far and not too fast."

"Excellent. See if you can catch me, Quinten Stone. If you do, maybe I'll wash a few spots for *you*." Katie took off jogging, no doubt taking Quin by surprise. But if she did surprise him, he didn't waste any time playing catch-up.

When she glanced over her shoulder, Quin was closing the distance she had put between them. The masculine scowl on his face sent a trickle of excitement down her spine. He looked predatory, determined.

Katie was running faster than she had planned. Suddenly, she remembered Farrell telling her about Quin's intensity, his laser focus. The way he pushed and pushed until he achieved his goals.

Only right now, Quin was supposed to be taking it easy. For a few more weeks. So his body could heal.

Katie stopped dead in the middle of the path. People went around her as if she were an island parting a river into two streams. She put her hands to her cheeks. "I am so sorry, Quin. I wasn't thinking. It was a game. But I don't want you to get hurt. Not again."

He pulled up short, right in front of her. Practically nose to nose. He slid his hands into her hair, tipped her head back, smashed his mouth over hers. "You make me crazy, Katie Duncan."

Frustration vibrated in his big frame. She could *feel* his turmoil.

Was that why she had run? Not a game at all, but a ploy to be chased? Captured? Subdued?

"Ditto, Quin." She wrapped her arms around his neck. "I don't even know what I'm doing anymore. We're supposed to be *working*."

He nuzzled her nose with his. "Not on the weekend. Everybody deserves a couple of days off."

"You're one of the big bosses. I suppose you could take off any day you want to… Isn't that where the term *playboy* comes from? A rich guy who can pilot a yacht or fly a helicopter or…" She trailed off, realizing she had backed herself into a corner.

Quin lifted a shoulder and let it fall, his expression wry. "Or ski down a mountain?"

Eleven

Quin released Katie and took her hand, linking his fingers with hers. The quarter-mile walk back to the hotel was both silent and peaceful. He rarely spent a day as relaxed as this one. Even when he was skiing, he was setting goals and sailing past them.

At the Carlyle, he and Katie took the elevator up to their floor. Again, silence reigned. What was she thinking? What did she want?

He regretted not getting to know her better when they were dating two years ago. Instead, he had explored the mutual hunger that drew them like two strong magnets, one to the other.

In the suite, he touched her shoulder. "You ready for dessert?"

She put her hand over his, warm brown eyes signaling her intent. "I'd like a shower. With you."

She was direct. Not coy. Not making him guess. He swallowed hard, his hands trembling. "I like the sound of that."

He couldn't put his finger on how things had changed, but they had. Their sojourn in the park had affected them both. The mood was more comfortable now, but no less sexually charged.

In the bathroom, Katie stripped off her clothes casually. Quin started the shower and adjusted the water. As she stepped into the roomy enclosure, Quin got naked as quickly as he could.

When he joined Katie, she averted her gaze, her posture wary. Pale blond hair turned rich gold as the water saturated the long strands. While he watched, Katie reached up with two hands and sluiced the water from her face, taming her soaked hair into a rich waterfall.

Though he wasn't sure, it seemed as if her hands trembled. "Are you nervous, Kat?" he asked. "We left the light on. It's still not dark outside. We can't blame this one on late-night debauchery."

"I know. And yes, I'm nervous. I'm always nervous around you. It's like throwing a baby doll into a moat with an alligator. You're always going to come out on top."

"Is that a loaded metaphor?"

"No. Just the truth. You and I are very different, Quin."

He opened a small bottle of shower gel. The heavy

scent of jasmine filled the steamy enclosure. "Turn around," he said gruffly.

When she tugged her hair forward over her shoulder and gave him her back, he was struck by how vulnerable she looked. How beautifully feminine the nape of her neck was. How trim her waist. Softly rounded hips flared just enough for a man to grasp.

He'd been hard since she kicked off her running shoes and bared her narrow feminine feet with the high arches and perfectly polished toes. Instead of pouncing on her as his libido urged, he dug deep and found tenderness. Gentle care. The other was coming, but not yet.

Doing her back was tricky. He had lathered up a washcloth, but when he touched her, the practical aspects of the chore got derailed by the need to linger. Both shoulders demanded his attention. Then the shoulder blades. Before moving south, he remembered to wash her neck.

Katie stood perfectly still, almost as if she was holding her breath. He squatted and washed her round ass, her thighs, her legs. He was breathing hard now, his heart pounding against his rib cage.

"Turn around," he said hoarsely.

Now he was on eye level with her pink, perfect sex. He traced her center with one fingertip. Katie shifted restlessly.

He lurched to his feet and washed her breasts. One at a time. Trying not to lose focus when he saw how the soap bubbles glistened—then eventually slid—over her heated skin.

When he moved toward her navel, Katie grabbed his wrist. Hard. "Are we doing this right here?" she asked, the words barely audible. Tendrils of damp hair clung to her forehead. Her eyelashes were spiky.

He leaned down and kissed her nose. "Ladies' choice."

The tiniest of smiles tilted her lips. "And if I don't feel like being a lady tonight?"

His sex, already fully erect, tightened painfully. "Um…" His throat closed up and his legs threatened to wobble.

She put her hands on his wet shoulders and pushed. "Sit down, Quin."

He lost his balance and plopped down hard on the narrow shower bench. Katie straddled his legs.

"Wait," he said wheezing for breath. "We don't have a con—"

She put her hand over his mouth. "Relax. I'm just playing with you. Any objections?"

"None," he croaked.

Katie sat down carefully. Now his erection nestled between them. He wasn't at all sure this was a good idea, but he sure as hell wasn't going to stop her.

"You are a sexy guy, Quin," she said. "Did you know that?"

"Um…" Apparently this shower interlude was adversely affecting his vocabulary. And he was pretty sure this was a trick question. It seemed better not to answer.

She ran her thumbs across his eyelids, forcing him to shut them. Now his other senses were heightened. He felt the steam that moistened their skin. He smelled Katie's warm, wet closeness.

"Keep your eyes closed, Quin," she said.

"Yes, ma'am." Before he could guess what she was going to do next, she took his hands and put them on her breasts.

Damn that was good. He pushed both mounds together and buried his face in the fragrant valley.

Katie muttered something he couldn't decipher. She leaned into him. "I like that," she whispered. "A lot."

He was blind. Moving along in the darkness. The wanting in his gut became a living torment. Lust roiled in his belly. He tasted her nipples. She was sweet and tart and *exactly right for him*.

The random thought both shocked and terrified him. Katie was the kind of woman who would marry a regular guy, a man who would give her babies and a house in the suburbs. Quin would never be a good father, maybe no father at all. What did he know about kids or security?

His childhood had been crap. No home-baked cookies. No bedtime stories. No warm, loving hugs during a thunderstorm or a nightmare.

She had been right to walk away from him.

Katie bit his earlobe, pulling him back into the moment. He grabbed her ass. "You know I like your teasing, Kat, but I'm *not* made of stone. You're killing me. I need to be inside you."

"Soon. I want what you want, Quin." She stroked his hair with gentle repetitive motions that in another context would have been soothing. He was so wired and on edge, even the nonsexual touch was painfully arousing.

"We're done here," he groaned. He scooted her off his lap and stood, wrapping his arm around her waist. "Bed," he muttered.

Katie rebelled. "No, please. You'll get the sheets all wet."

"Fine." He grabbed a towel, dragged her with him into the bedroom, and despite his weak knee, scooped her up and dumped her on the settee. "Don't move."

Katie's eyes were huge. Had she really expected him to remain passive under such provocation? He rummaged for more of the protection he had bought that morning.

When he saw how she stared at him, he faltered. "Am I going too fast, Kat?"

She chewed her lip. "No. Your brothers told me how controlled you are. Seeing you snap is kind of flattering."

He ripped open a packet and rolled the condom onto his shaft. "You've made me lose control since the first day I bumped into you at the water cooler. Literally. You were wearing a pale pink sundress. Your hair was up. I think the earrings were sterling silver stars." Her look of incredulity amused him. "Why is that so surprising?"

"You're exaggerating about the control thing."

He came down beside her and lifted her leg to the back of the velvet-covered furniture, stroking her thigh. "No. Not even a little." Their bodies struggled in the awkward arrangement. No room to maneuver. Katie didn't seem to mind. He entered her slowly, holding her bottom in one hand and bracing himself with the other. "I'm glad you came to Maine, Kat. It's been pretty dark since the accident. You've dragged me out of the pit, I think."

"Don't talk," she begged. "Take me hard."

"Yes. Yes." It was an easy request to grant. He tried to make it last. He really did. But it had been hours since he'd made love to her. Her arms wrapped around his neck, threatening to choke him. She linked her ankles at his back, her heels digging into his waist.

"Ah, hell." He came in minutes, his mind blank with stunned pleasure. The end went on forever. Little aftershocks that left him dizzy and spent. He lifted away and pleasured her with his touch, groaning with relief when she came wildly, crying out his name.

When he could breathe, he surveyed the situation. "We're all dry now. Bed?"

She nodded, her eyes closed. "You're the boss."

Katie slept like the dead for hours. In fact, she would have happily slept longer if not for an annoying beep nearby. Grumbling and shifting to squint at her surroundings, she poked Quin. "Is that a smoke alarm?"

He lifted onto one elbow, bleary-eyed. "Phone alarm." His voice was hoarse with fatigue. That's what happened when two otherwise sane adults chose to fornicate like rabbits instead of getting the eight solid hours of sleep recommended by the American Medical Association.

"Why in God's name did you set an alarm?"

"We have to fly home," he muttered.

"You're a billionaire. It's a private plane. Tell him we'll be ready midafternoon."

"Can't. Flight plan's already been filed. Gotta go…"

She stumbled to the bathroom and did the best she could. When they left the hotel forty-five minutes later, she pondered the inequities of life. Katie could barely look at herself in the mirror as they sailed through the lobby. Her hair was on top of her head in a messy knot. She still had pillow creases on her face, and the dark circles under her eyes were epic.

Quin, on the other hand, looked like the image of a wealthy, handsome bachelor enjoying a relaxing day off. He had topped his snug heather-gray T-shirt with a loose khaki linen jacket. His jeans were exactly the right amount of *worn*, and the shadow of dark stubble on his gorgeous chin made him look sexy and dangerous.

Their hired car waited at the curb. Quin tucked her in and ran around to the street side. Thank God it was Sunday. The usual morning traffic insanity was subdued.

All the way to the airport, through takeoff and during the brief flight north, Katie knew something had changed. It was possible that Quin's slightly aloof attitude was merely exhaustion. She might be reading too much into his silence. The fact that he was skimming the news on his iPad instead of flirting with her was nothing sinister.

Katie leaned her seat back and dozed during the relatively brief flight. Mrs. Peterson met them at the landing strip in a Jeep. The luggage was loaded in the back, and soon, Katie was climbing the front steps of Quin's house… Right where she had started.

Quin smiled at the housekeeper. "Thanks for coming in today. Why don't you go on home and take tomorrow off?"

"Thank you, Mr. Quin," she said. "There's plenty for lunch and dinner in the fridge. You can pick and choose. I left the cooking and warming instructions on the island."

"Sounds great."

The older woman paused. "I don't mean to be pushy, but we may be in for a serious summer storm. I stocked the pantry just in case, and the generators have been serviced. You and Miss Katie should really take a look at the weather forecast."

Quin groaned. "Zachary said something similar on Friday. So it's taking shape?"

"Looks that way." Her matter-of-fact answer made Katie smile inwardly. Folks in Maine took bad weather in stride. Still, there had been a few very destructive storms over the years.

"In that case," Quin said, "Don't come back out here until you hear from me, one way or the other. You'll have preparations to make at your own home. Katie and I will be fine."

"Okay, then. Let me finish tidying the kitchen, and I'll be off."

When the older woman walked away, an awkward silence fell. Was Quin regretting the indulgent weekend he and Katie had spent in New York? Had too many barriers been crossed? Maybe he wanted to go back to the boss/employee relationship.

Hurt curled in Katie's stomach. The man with whom she had shared a bed—and various other real estate—was not the same man who stood before her now. Quin's gaze was shuttered, his jaw tight.

He hunched his shoulders, not quite meeting her gaze. "It's Sunday. We're not going to work today. Why don't you relax and get some fresh air? We may be cooped up in the house for a couple of days. You might as well enjoy yourself while the sun is shining."

She couldn't decide how to respond to that, and it didn't really matter, because Quin gave her a terse nod and walked in the direction of the makeshift office they shared.

Her eyes burned, and her throat was tight. Was he being a jerk on purpose, or had something upset him? Did the reason matter? Clearly, their wonderful weekend was over.

She took her bags up to her room, dumped them on the bed and changed into comfortable clothes. Though she had been living at Quin's home for several weeks now, she had only surveyed the ocean from higher ground. Today she was in a mind to find the water's edge and drown her sorrows. The bad joke didn't even lift her mood.

The path down to the beach was not well marked. The jumble of boulders had been there for millennia, occasionally tossed about by rough seas. The narrow trail *existed*, but it was fairly treacherous. She was forced to pick her way carefully or risk breaking an ankle.

The challenge was worth it. By the time she made it onto the narrow strip of sand, her heart was racing, but her state of mind had lightened fractionally. She sat on a rock and removed her socks. The sand was cool beneath her feet.

It seemed impossible that a storm was in the offing. The sea today was a deep, placid turquoise, calm enough to soothe her fear of water. Small pools held sea creatures trapped by low tide. She examined each one, charmed by the diversity. Crabs and starfish, hot pink seaweed and deep red anemones. Even a sea urchin or two. Kneeling in the sand, she used her phone to snap a few pictures.

The creepiest thing she found was a slithery eel-like animal, which she absolutely *didn't* touch. There was even the tiniest of baby lobsters. Why that surprised her, she couldn't say. Obviously, lobsters weren't born being huge and meaty. They had to start small sometime.

She found a measure of peace in the rich beauty of nature. Even if things had soured with Quin, at least she could enjoy her time here. Though she had lived in Maine her entire life, Portland was a far cry from this wild northern coastline. Her parents had barely fed their family. Leisure trips to the shore, even for the day, were few and far between.

When she tired of exploring, she rolled up her pants legs to brave the water. The breeze had begun to pick up, whipping the surface of the ocean into frothy whitecaps. Her toes curled. Maybe this was a bad idea. Strong currents swept this part of the coast.

Not that she was going for a swim. She just wanted to be able to say she had waded in the Atlantic. And to prove that her long-standing fear of water hadn't crippled her.

The noise of the waves masked other sounds.

When a male voice spoke behind her, it was like that first day all over again. She whirled and nearly fell on her butt.

Quin chuckled. "I didn't mean to scare you. How long have you been down here?"

She shot him a wary glance over her shoulder, distrusting his whiplash mood changes. "I don't know. An hour…maybe two." Suddenly she looked up at the path to the house. "I don't think you're supposed to be doing something like this. The doctor said *gentle* exercise."

"I've climbed down this path a hundred times."

"Since the accident?"

Twelve

Quin frowned. "I'm capable of monitoring my own fitness. I've been doing it since I was a teenager. If I had thought following you down to the ocean would negatively impact my knee, I wouldn't have come."

"That's not what your brothers say. They tell me you test your limits. Sometimes with painful results."

"That was the old Quin. I'm a reformed man." He said it lightly, but it was true in a way. He'd learned some hard lessons during the last two years.

Katie turned back to the ocean. "You're very lucky to live here," she said. "I was just about to stick my feet in the water. An homage to summer."

"It will be a shock," he said. "The water temperature is barely sixty degrees."

"I can handle it." She struck out immediately, halting when the water hit just below her knees. "Oh gosh."

"I warned you."

Katie wrapped her arms around her waist. Her hair began to come loose from its knot now that the wind had picked up.

She was guarded in her posture. No wonder. He'd been deliberately aloof earlier. Coming back to Maine had shocked him into a realization of what he was doing. Katie claimed to want only three weeks in his bed. But did he himself want more?

"Come sit on the rocks with me," he cajoled. "They're warm from the sun. You need to thaw out."

Thirty seconds passed. Then a whole minute. Finally, Katie turned around and slogged back to shore.

Her teeth were chattering. "I love the ocean," she said.

"But maybe Florida is more your speed?"

He was teasing. Katie took him seriously. "Oh no," she said, rolling down her pant legs and perching beside him. "I love the peace and the isolation here. I'm not a fan of crowded beaches. At least I don't think I would be. My family hasn't traveled much. My parents both had jobs where they didn't get paid if they didn't work, so no trips south for us. And to be honest, hot weather isn't really my thing."

"You said *had* jobs. Have they already retired?"

"Sort of...they sold their house in Portland and found a mobile home in Myrtle Beach. Not 'on' the beach, of course. They're just happy to be away from winters in Maine. They've found part-time work in South Carolina that helps pay the bills."

"Is their move why your sister is looking for an apartment? Didn't she live with them?"

"Yes."

"And what about the loser boyfriend? Is he still in the picture?"

Katie had one foot propped on a smaller rock. Her hands were linked around her knee. "I'm not comfortable talking to you about Jimmy," she said. "Let's change the subject, please." The words were curt.

He deserved that. Katie's sister's boyfriend had sparked one of the biggest fights Quin and Katie ever had. He sighed inwardly. "I'm sorry."

"Did you check the forecast?" she asked, not acknowledging his apology.

"I did. They're expecting the storm to be a strong category three as it scrapes over the Outer Banks. Then it will track like Sandy did or Bob in '91. We'll get some damage for sure, but not catastrophic."

"I thought Maine was mostly hurricane-proof, because of the cold ocean waters."

"Technically true, but even a tropical storm can bring down trees."

"Are you worried?"

"No. If a hurricane makes it to Maine, it's usually downgraded rapidly." He put his arm around her shoulders and kissed her cheek. "You don't have to be afraid, Katie. I would never let anything happen to you, I swear."

"I'm not worried, Quin." Her body was stiff at

first, but gradually, she relaxed. They sat in silence, enjoying the perfect afternoon. Trouble would come soon enough.

Being near her like this produced an odd mix of reactions in his gut. He wanted her. He was beginning to think he would never *not* want her. Even more than that—at least for now—he found himself surprisingly content. Almost alarmingly happy.

It had been a hell of a long time since he had experienced either of those emotions.

"I think I know why you broke up with me," he said.

"Oh?" Katie's reaction was hard to miss. He was holding her closely. Her body leaned into his. Right up until the moment he spoke those ten words. She jumped to her feet and went back to the water's edge. If he wasn't mistaken, the tide was about to turn.

When she didn't say anything else, he sighed inwardly. Maybe this was a bad idea. But he had started down this road and there was no room to turn around. "You wanted a family someday," he said. "And I was a guy with no roots. Just a passport and a determination to make it to the next city, the next tournament. Am I right?"

He joined her for a second time.

She nodded slowly. "That was part of it. But I wanted to know you. Really know you. And I wanted you to know me. You were so focused on your skiing that any woman who tried to fit into your life would always come in second place. Sometimes I think you were more emotionally connected to your stupid mountains than you were to me."

He grimaced. "You weren't wrong," he said quietly. "I was obsessed, determined to make it to that elusive first place podium before I hung up my skis. My plan was to continue competing until I was at least thirty-five, maybe longer. That seems laughable now."

"I'm sorry, Quin. I really am. You were so good at what you did and so buoyed by that dream. Is there even a tiny chance that you can go back to the World Cup alpine circuit, maybe as an experiment?"

"None. I would only embarrass myself. As I said before, if I'm lucky, and if I don't do anything else stupid, the docs think that skiing for pleasure can definitely be part of my future."

"Will that be enough for you?"

"It will have to be." He paused. "Things are different now, Katie. *I'm* different now. Perhaps you and I could try again."

Still, she stared straight out to sea. Her cheeks were pink. It was hot in the full-on sun. Finally, she shot him a sideways glance, brown eyes judging him. "I don't think you realize how you sound, Quin. What you're saying is that I could be your consolation prize now that you've had to give up everything else you care about."

He winced. Was he really so clueless? "I didn't mean it like that," he muttered.

Katie laughed wryly. "I'm sure there are any number of women who would line up to take your mind off your troubles."

"You're the only one I want."

"At least for the moment. You told me you hadn't been with a woman since the accident. Was that true?"

His pride took a hit. "I am *not* a liar."

"Eighteen months. How is that possible? The Quin I knew could barely go eighteen *hours* without sex, much less eighteen months."

"I told you. I've changed."

"Why? How?"

Women always had to dig deeper. He didn't want to examine his inadequacies. Shoving his hands in his pockets, he squinted into the sun, looking for dolphins or the spume of a whale, anything to distract her.

"The car crash was bad. I was in and out of the hospital for weeks at a time. One of my incisions got infected. You saw me at the funeral home after Dad died. Those crutches? I was still using them months after the accident."

"Some women like nursing a wounded hero."

"I was surprised to see you at the service. For days afterward, I lay awake at night wondering what it meant."

She snorted softly. "It meant that I had sympathy for you and your brothers. Sorrow for your loss. It meant that the head of Stone River Outdoors was gone. It meant that I felt obligated to be there, *even though* I had to face you again."

"It had been six long months at that point," he said. "You avoided me at work. I wasn't stupid. I knew it."

"That's the downside of having an affair with the boss. When it ends, things get messy."

"And then—lucky for you—I was in a car crash, and you didn't have to worry anymore about bumping into me in the hallway."

Katie faced him, her expression stormy. "What a terrible thing to say. Maybe we weren't still together, but when I heard about the accident, it tore me up. It's true I didn't believe we had what it took to be a couple. I didn't hate you, though, Quin. I didn't want you to suffer."

"Gee, thanks."

"You didn't really answer my question. Why were there no women in your bed for a year and a half? I would have thought sex would take your mind off your troubles. A bit of oblivion occasionally."

"When life is reduced to its barest essentials, Kat, the truth becomes clear. I still wanted you."

Katie's heart jerked hard, then settled back into a boring rhythm. He was saying what he thought she wanted to hear. Surely, she wasn't going to be gullible enough to fall for his tempting exaggerations.

"It wasn't me," she insisted. "It's just that I represented a time *before* bad things happened to you. It was therapeutic to think about our affair."

"If you say so."

Goose bumps covered her bare arms. "I suppose we should go back to the house."

Quin stepped behind her and folded her in his arms. His big body radiated heat and a feeling of security. "You should gather your things and bring them down to my room. It will be safer to ride this thing out on the main floor. The wind will come off the water. My bedroom faces the forest."

"I bet you say that to all the girls," she teased.

He rested his chin on top of her head. His thumbs slipped under her shirt and caressed her belly. "There are two guest rooms on the first floor. You're welcome to the second one if you don't want to sleep with me."

Katie turned around and tipped back her head. Even then, she couldn't see the expression in his eyes. He wore expensive aviator sunglasses. "Don't play games with me, Quin. Admit it. You're not going to let me sleep in another room."

He shrugged. "I won't force the issue."

She cupped his sex through his pants. "Maybe I will."

Finally, the tension in his body relaxed. A sexy smile tilted his lips. "I like it when Kinky Kat comes out to play."

Beneath her fingers, his sex lifted and hardened. "I don't know about kinky," she said. "But I'm not dumb enough to give up having sex with you when we're living under the same roof. All our differences aside, we're good in bed, Quin. I can't deny that."

A tiny frown creased the space between his eyebrows. "Do you want to, Katie? Deny it, I mean?"

She chewed her lip. "It would be easier to walk away from you if there were no sparks. I'm as predictable as the next woman. When a hot guy wants to give me multiple orgasms, it's hard to say no."

"So you're using me?"

Was he serious? It was hard to tell. "I think we're using each other. And for the moment, I'm okay with that." She slid her hand into his and linked their fingers. "Come on. If I have to leave the guest suite and slum it downstairs, I'd better get to it. Besides, don't you have manly things to prepare? Generators and flashlights and all that disaster prep stuff guys like doing?"

He resisted her efforts to pull him toward the path. "Indeed, I do. But first things first." Before she could protest, he pulled every pin out of her lopsided topknot and tucked them in his pocket. Then he tunneled his fingers through her windblown hair and sighed. "New York was great, but I like having you under my roof."

He slanted his mouth over hers and took the kiss deep. Her toes curled into the sand. Her body heated from the inside out. The man was a fantastic kisser. *Really* good. Her hands clung to his shoulders.

When he released her, they were both breathing hard. He still wore those damned sunglasses. She reached up and removed them slowly. Brilliant blue eyes sizzled with heat.

"I'm a fan of good communication," she said. "For the record, I'm glad I'm here in Maine with you, Quinten."

He rubbed his thumb across her cheekbone. "Me, too, Kat. Me, too."

* * *

After she and Quin climbed back up from the beach, the remainder of the day passed uneventfully. They worked in tandem, making preparations for the storm to come. While Quin bungeed the outdoor rockers to the porch and secured other loose items, Katie moved her things downstairs.

The whole exercise felt oddly domestic, as if she was making the choice to move in with him. That wasn't exactly what was happening, but the situation was sexually charged, nevertheless. Sharing a hotel room with a lover was different than sharing a man's bedroom. Though she couldn't have explained why, it just *was*.

At dinnertime, Quin surprised her once again. She had assumed *she* would be the one in charge in the kitchen. Instead, Quin took over and put together an impressive meal of beef Stroganoff and Caesar salad with homemade bread. Admittedly, Mrs. Peterson had begun the preparations, but Quin handled himself in the kitchen as if he was comfortable there.

When she teased him about it, he shook his head. "Don't be sexist, Kat. It's the twenty-first century. I'm a single man. Of course, I cook a little. Most guys my age can throw together at least one or two decent meals."

"I suppose I thought you would order takeout when your housekeeper was off duty."

"Takeout? In the middle of the Maine woods?"

"Well, I hadn't seen your house at that point, now, had I? My vision of you is changing. You're a chameleon. I can't decide if you're a Thoreau wannabe who loves the hermit life or the world-weary jet-setter looking for the next big thrill ride."

He tweaked her nose and reached for a bottle of merlot, removing the cork with impressive ease. "Can't I be both?"

As he poured the wine and handed her a glass, Katie pondered his question. The truth was, she hadn't known Quin at all when they started dating. He'd been nothing but a name and a face to her—the youngest Stone sibling who was, more often than not, somewhere on the other side of the world.

It was only after his father's death that Quin had been handed the CEO job. A year or so before that, he had begun to take a more active role in the company, but even then, Katie had never met him up close and personal. Though she worked for Farrell, her path and Quin's had not crossed in any kind of meaningful way. It was that weird quirk of fate at the communal water fountain that had thrown them together.

Now, here she was.

As they sat down to eat, she noted the flickering lights. "Do you think we'll lose power soon?"

"The generator is hardwired into the house...runs off propane. But even though I have a large tank, if we have severe storm damage, we could be stranded for days. We'll want to be cautious in the beginning."

Thirteen

Quin could see on Katie's face that she hadn't thought through the implications of the upcoming storm. It was one thing to get clobbered in a city where fire and police and emergency responders would immediately start working to repair infrastructure. Where Quin and his brothers lived, they were miles from the nearest house.

Their needs would fall way down the list. As they should.

He paused to kiss his cute houseguest on the cheek before setting the salad bowls on the table and waving her to a seat. "Don't worry, Kat. We'll be fine. It's summer. If we have to, we can sleep outside when it gets too hot."

"Oh goody," she said, wrinkling her nose.

What struck him during the intimate dinner was how the conversation never lagged. Katie always referenced how good they were in bed, and damn, that was true, but Quin also knew that he'd met few women who challenged him on an intellectual and emotional level the way Katie did. He found himself wanting to be a better man when they were together.

"I have a surprise for you, Kat," he said, finishing off the last bite of apple pie.

"Oh?"

"Farrell and Zachary and I have been putting together a scholarship program for young people whose parents work for Stone River Outdoors. We want to make sure every kid who wants a college education can get one."

She beamed at him. "That's wonderful! Let me know if I can help with any of the paperwork."

"I might take you up on that. And we're also setting up a family relief fund. For the kinds of emergencies that drag people under. Any employee can apply and get help, depending upon the severity of the situation and how long they have worked for the company."

Katie came and wrapped her arms around his neck from behind. "I'm so proud of you," she said, brushing a kiss at his nape.

He shivered and caught her hands in his. "It's all because of you, Katie. When we were together, you kept ragging my butt about how my family's wealth was a great responsibility and how I needed to keep perspective about the world. You wanted me to always be aware of how much I have and how little others get by with. I heard you, Kat. Loud and clear."

She released him and sat down again, her gaze troubled. "Am I really such a sanctimonious prig? I'm sorry. I didn't mean to be. You should have told me to shut up. It wasn't my place to criticize."

He stood and began clearing the table. "It was a much-needed wake-up call for me. My father was not a generous man at all. *Charity* was never a word he taught us. But we're all grown men now, and I'm determined not to follow in his footsteps."

Katie's smile of approval warmed him. She began to help him with the dishes, but her cell phone rang. She glanced at the number, and her demeanor changed visibly. "Excuse me," she said, her face flushing. "I need to take this in the other room."

She didn't go far. Only out in the hallway. Quin didn't eavesdrop intentionally, but it was hard not to overhear.

Katie lowered her voice and answered the call. "Delanna. What's up?"

Her sister's voice had that squeaky note that always preceded a request. "I know you're helping me with all my utility deposits," Delanna said, "but I could really use a couple hundred more to get a few things I need. I'll pay you back, I swear. I'm just a little short right now."

"Delanna." Katie screwed up her courage. She hated these confrontations. "Are you giving part of my money to Jimmy?"

Long silence. "Why would you say that?"

"Because he always begs, and you roll over. I've helped him again and again. You know he's an addict. He's not going to change."

"He's trying, Katie, I swear he is. He just got out of jail this past weekend. He's been sober for three straight weeks."

"Until you hand over enough cash for him to hit up his dealer."

"Why are you being so mean?"

"I'm not mean, sis. But you're enabling him. You deserve better. I've done everything I can to help both of you, but I'm tired of being an ATM. You have a good job and a place to live. Please don't let Jimmy drag you down a dead-end road."

"I don't even know why I called," Delanna said, her tone indignant. "You think you're better than everybody else, don't you?"

The jab hurt, particularly after the recent conversation with Quin. Katie's throat tightened. "I'm sorry you feel that way. I have to go. Take care during the storm."

Katie tried blinking back the tears, but they spilled over. Lifting the hem of her shirt, she dried her face and took a deep breath. Had she done the right thing?

She leaned against the wall and thought about everything Quin had said. He really *was* changing. Was she the one who needed a wake-up call now?

When she was relatively calm, she returned to the kitchen.

Quin looked up when she entered. "Everything okay?"

She wanted desperately to bury her face in his chest and let him comfort her. But she was too embarrassed to talk about the current situation. Quin had been so vehement in the past about her penchant for rescuing her family and especially Jimmy.

Would the new Quin be any more receptive? His father's interference hung in the balance, as well. Katie wanted to unburden herself, but was it fair to dump the whole truth on Quin? It was bound to hurt him, or make him angry, or both.

She swallowed her desperation and her disappointment. "Everything is fine. I was thinking it would be fun to go outside for a bit. While we still can."

He dried his big masculine hands on a dish towel. "Whatever you want, Kat." How such a simple motion seemed so sexy, she couldn't say, but she melted inside.

They ended up sitting barefoot on the top step of the front porch, looking for stars. Earlier, on the beach, the sky had been clear all the way to the horizon. Now clouds were already rolling in.

When Quin moved, it took Katie by surprise. He laid her back on the porch so gently she barely noticed the hard boards beneath her back. She cleared her throat. "What are you up to, Quin?"

It was hard to read his expression, but the amusement in his husky voice came through loud and clear. "If you have to ask, I'm probably not doing it right." He leaned over her and kissed her. "I'm all for modern conveniences, but the idea of making love to you by candlelight during a storm has a definite appeal, my Kat."

He pressed a second kiss to her throat, right where the shallow dip of her top bared her skin. Then he moved to the shell of her ear, his breath warm and scented with wine.

Katie's lungs struggled for oxygen. "The storm hasn't started yet," she muttered. The stars began moving in dizzying arcs. "Do you even own any candles?" That sound she heard was embarrassing. A cross between a ragged moan and a plea. Definitely her voice, not Quin's.

He chuckled, though he was breathing awfully hard for a man who was sitting still. Her activewear pants had an elastic waist. Quin's big hand trespassed beneath the band. His fingers splayed against her stomach. His thumb inched south.

"You can tell me to stop, Kat. I have several good beds inside the house. I could take you in every single one if you like."

She urged him lower—telepathically—but he didn't get the hint. "Do you have protection? Here? Outside?"

That frustrating thumb moved another millimeter in the right direction. With his free hand, he delved into his pocket. "Actually, I do." He waved the strip of packets in the air.

Katie wanted to laugh, but she could barely breathe. "Okay, then."

He tugged her to her feet. "I want you naked, Kat.

There's no one here to see us but the coyotes and the raccoons."

Her nerve endings felt both numb and tingly at the same time. Quin wasted no time in dispensing with her shirt and bra. Her pants and undies met the same fate. Suddenly, she found herself bare-assed naked.

While Quin stripped off his own clothes, Katie wrapped her arms around her breasts. He possessed not one ounce of self-consciousness about being nude outdoors. She, on the other hand, felt exposed. As if at any moment a helicopter might hover overhead and pin them down with a giant spotlight.

Quin read her nervousness. "We're alone, Katie. Relax."

"I'm trying, believe me."

He sat down on the top step and patted his knees. "Come here, beautiful woman. Let me hold you."

At first, she wasn't exactly sure what he was suggesting. A sexy cuddle? Something more?

He didn't leave her in suspense. He tugged her ankle. "Straddle me. Before we get serious."

She gulped inwardly. *This* wasn't serious? Moments later, he moved her into position, his erect sex between them in the V of her legs.

Quin smoothed his hands over her bottom, squeezing.

Katie grimaced, though she doubted he noticed. "I could stand to lose a few pounds."

"Women are so dumb." He repeated that same motion, caressing her ass, stoking the fire in her abdomen until she squirmed.

"It's not nice to call me dumb."

"Then don't criticize your body again. I happen to like it exactly as it is. Soft and curvy and perfect."

The utter sincerity in his voice seduced her as surely as his magic touch. Did he really believe that? She was just an ordinary woman.

He leaned his forehead against hers. "What are you thinking about? I can tell when you zone out on me."

"Sorry." She slid her fingers through his silky hair, tracing the lines of his skull, playing with his ears. "I was wondering how long you were going to make me wait."

His breathless laugh held equal parts humor and male satisfaction. "Soon, Kat. Soon." He leaned back on his hands. "Touch your breasts."

"Excuse me?" Her sex tightened.

"You heard what I said. Touch your breasts. I want to watch."

Her mouth gaped. They had never played these kinds of games. Not two years ago, and certainly not since she had come to Maine. Did he think she was too inhibited to meet his challenge?

The night air was cool on her heated skin. The way she was sitting made her feel open. Exposed. Stingingly vulnerable. Already she was hungry for him. Damp. Needy.

Slowly, she lifted her arms and cupped her hands around her breasts. His muffled curse emboldened her. "Like this?"

There was enough ambient light from inside the house for him to see her every move, especially now

that their eyes had grown accustomed to the dark.
She squeezed and plumped her own curves, deepen-
ing the valley between them. With her thumbs, she
fondled her own nipples.

Quin sat up abruptly. "That's enough," he said
gruffly.

"Why? This feels so good."

He grabbed her wrists and held them away from
her body, then leaned in and suckled her breasts one
at a time. His teeth raked sensitive flesh. His tongue
left her skin sheened with moisture. When the wind
picked up, gooseflesh covered her body. The ache in
her pelvis deepened to the point of pain.

She struggled. "I want you," she cried.

Quin cursed and reached for a condom, rolling it
on with a single smooth movement that left her in awe
of his grace. "You've got me, Kat." He lifted her with
two strong arms and settled her onto his erection.

The slide of soft female sheath against hard male
shaft was more than she had expected. Every time
with Quin was different now. As if they were climbing a scale she couldn't see. Had it been this good
before? Or was the long time they spent apart mag-
nifying her reaction to him?

"Don't stop," she whispered. He felt huge inside
her. The sensation was incredible.

"You're in this, too, Kat. Ride me, sweetheart."

She felt embarrassed at first. What did she know
about pleasing a man like Quin? She was *not* sexually adventurous. But what if she concentrated on
pleasing herself?

Slowly she slid upward until their bodies were barely joined. Her bare feet felt chilled on the wooden steps. Any residual heat from the day was gone. Her hands ended up on Quin's shoulders. For balance.

She could actually hear his labored breathing and feel the rigid strain in his arms. "Now?" she asked, teasing.

He nodded, mute. Palpably desperate.

When she pushed downward, Quin groaned softly.

With her thigh muscles protesting the unaccustomed exercise, she rode him slowly, torturing both of them with the exquisite pleasure. Up and down. Take and retreat.

Why didn't men and women have sex outdoors more often? This was amazing. She felt free and wild. And though her climax rushed down the pike, she held it off, wanting more of this sweet, wanton experience.

Quin's hands were everywhere. Stroking her back. Gripping her butt. Sliding into her hair and dragging her close for hungry kisses.

If she listened hard enough, she could hear past the sounds of their bodies connecting forcefully. In the distance, an owl hooted a mournful cry. The rising wind bent the trees and made a song of branch and twig.

Quin buried his face between her breasts and kissed her curves, over and around, up and down. "Damn, woman. You're killing me."

She cupped his face in her hands, trying desperately to read his expression. "What a way to go," she whispered.

In that instant, she felt a sharp spike of grief. She loved him. Deeply. Irrevocably. What was she going to do with that information?

He shifted his hips and thrust upward, deliberately holding her against the base of his sex. The extra stimulation sent her reeling. Her cry of completion echoed on the breeze. The orgasm went on and on, both terrifying and electrifying. She had no defenses against this. Against him.

Whatever happened would happen. She no longer had the strength to fight the pull he exerted over her emotions, her life.

Quin held her close as she shuddered in his arms. "Will you be okay with me on top, Kat?"

She nodded, lax with pleasure. "What's a few butt splinters between friends?"

His chuckle was raspy. "That's my girl." Carefully, he disengaged their connection and laid her back on the porch once again. With her knees bent, her feet rested on the first step.

Quin moved over her and into her. His guttural moan when he shoved all the way to her cervix made the hair stand up on her arms. She wanted to say something, but her throat had closed, swollen with impossible, careening emotions.

As she held him tightly, he found his own release. His body was beautiful in its power and dominance.

She stroked his hair for hours, it seemed, listening

as his galloping heartbeat finally settled back into an ordinary rhythm.

When he finally moved, it was to lift up onto one hand and swipe his face with the other. "Are you cold, Kat?"

She nodded slowly. "Yes. Let's go to your bed."

Fourteen

When Quin thought his legs would support him, he stood and held out a hand to Katie. "No need to get dressed. We might as well shower and hit the sack. The next forty-eight hours may be challenging."

He winced inwardly. What kind of asshat lover discussed the weather after a cataclysm like that?

Despite his clumsy segue, Katie followed his lead. They each gathered up their own clothes. Once they were inside, he locked the front door and set the alarm. When he turned around, Katie was already halfway down the hall, her cute, naked, heart-shaped backside drawing his gaze.

When he entered the bedroom, she bent and took a T-shirt and underwear out of her suitcase. "I'll shower first," she said, not meeting his gaze.

Though he had a quip at the ready, his tongue wouldn't work. His lips couldn't form the words. He and Katie had moved into some new dimension he didn't recognize. Maybe it was only the newness of the situation. Tonight was auspicious. His Kat was going to share *his* bed.

When she exited the bathroom, he strode past her, pretending he didn't notice the way her casual nightwear made her look like an innocent college girl ready to cuddle with her favorite teddy bear.

The thought of sleeping with her all night and again tomorrow and the next night and the next threw him off balance. What were these odd feelings assailing him? His beautiful home was possibly about to get pounded by a tropical storm. He had finally accepted that his professional skiing career was over. Someone might have tried to kill his father and Quin both.

As he examined his current life, there was damned little to be glad about. Yet here he was, grinning inside, because the woman he wanted was climbing into his king-size bed.

His shower was hot and quick. He toweled off, inhaling the scent of Katie in his bathroom. When he was dry, he wrapped another towel around his hips. No sense in tempting fate by waltzing out of the bathroom naked. He and Katie had been up early and had a very long day. He would let her sleep... If he could.

When he returned to the bedroom, all the lights were off except for the two small bedside lamps that cast a cozy but narrow glow. Katie was propped up against the headboard with a pile of pillows, reading a paperback novel. Mystery? Romance? Grisly police procedural? He couldn't be sure, because she slipped it under the sheet.

"That was fast," she said, her smile shy.

He shrugged, dropped the towel and climbed into bed. "I didn't want to waste any time getting back to my best girl."

She rolled her eyes. "Are we going to the sock hop after we stop at the soda fountain?"

"Don't make fun of me." He dragged her closer and kissed her slowly, smiling when she melted against him.

Her arms went around his neck. "Are we really having sex again?" Her yawn was either genuine or for effect. He couldn't tell.

"Fix your pillows, woman. We're going to sleep."

She gave him a mock salute. "Yes, sir."

When they were both settled under the covers, he spooned her. His yawn was definitely the real deal. "This is nice, Kat."

"Ditto, Quin."

The last thing he remembered was Katie lacing her fingers with his and sighing as they both crashed into unconsciousness.

Quin jerked awake at 5:00 a.m., sickly certain that something was wrong. He reached for his phone, rolled away from Katie so the screen wouldn't disturb her and checked the weather. His heart sank and fear dug claws into his gut. He wasn't worried about himself, but he couldn't let anything happen to Katie, not when she had come to Maine so cheerfully to be of service to the Stone family in general and Quin in particular.

Despite his careful silence, his movements in the bed must have disturbed her. She raised up on one elbow and shoved the hair out of her face. "What is it? What's wrong?"

He set the phone aside. "Go back to sleep. We'll deal with it in the morning."

Fortunately, Katie was too tired to argue. In moments, she was breathing deeply again. Quin wasn't so lucky.

Eventually, exhaustion claimed him, despite his unease.

When morning finally dawned, he slid out of bed, threw on sweatpants and padded to the living room. Might as well use the TV while they still had it. Soon, the outside world would be a mystery.

The news was about as bad as it could be for the Pine Tree State. Hurricanes always lost power over these colder waters, but Tropical Storm Figaro was bearing down on coastal Maine with a vengeance. It had picked up speed during the night, wreaking havoc all over the mid-Atlantic seaboard and getting ready to pound southern New England.

Katie appeared in the doorway. She crossed the room and curled up in his lap. "How long do we have?" she asked.

She still smelled like his bed, her body warm and cuddly in his embrace. His arm tightened around her.

"Hard to say. We'll probably get hit with the worst of it around midnight, give or take."

"I hate having storms at night. It's not so scary in the daytime. I want to see what's coming for me."

He grinned. "Don't tell me you want to stand out on the rocky overlook and let the spray wash over you?"

"If I had a guarantee that I wouldn't get hurt, I would *love* to experience a storm like that. The power and the fury of Mother Nature. It has a certain appeal."

"You're a crazy woman. I like it." He picked up the remote and silenced the TV. "No sense in depressing ourselves. We might as well carry on as usual until dinnertime."

"I agree." She stood and stretched. "I'm very close to finishing two time-sensitive reports. I'd feel a lot better if I got those done."

"Sounds good. When you're finished, how about filling all the bathtubs with water. And the sinks, too. We can boil water later, but we'll need a supply. I'm going to make sure I haven't missed anything outside. All the vehicles are in the garage. I found a spot for yours, too. And don't forget to charge your devices."

Katie wrinkled her nose. "This is really happening, isn't it?"

When Katie disappeared to get dressed, Quin called Farrell. "Where are you, buddy?"

His older brother sounded stressed. "I'm still in Portland. Zach is, too. We shut down the plant and the office building this morning. Sent everyone home.

It's too late for us to come north now. I hired a local guy to head up to my place and Zachary's and do basic storm prep."

Quin frowned, though Farrell couldn't see the grimace. "I'd have been happy to handle that for both of you."

"I know. But you're supposed to be taking it easy for a little bit longer. I'm sure you're tied up with taking care of your own place. Did Katie decide to go home?"

Quin felt his face heat. He'd never even contemplated that. "No," he said. "She's still here."

Long silence. Farrell sighed. "Tell her to call me, and I'll stop by her condo this afternoon."

"You and Zachary hunker down."

"You, too. I don't imagine cell service will survive. We'll check on you when we can. Love you, bro."

"Same here."

"Quin?"

"Yeah?"

"What's the story with Katie? I'd like to have my A.A. back sooner than later. Please don't screw with her."

"I'm guessing you don't mean that literally."

Farrell muttered a curse. "I didn't, but I do now. Be smart about this, man. Katie is important to Stone River Outdoors."

"She's important to me, too." Quin sat down hard on the arm of the sofa. Saying those words had him feeling a little dizzy and a lot queasy. He wasn't ill. But he sure as hell was confused.

"I've never heard you say that about *any* woman," Farrell said, his tone a combination of shock and concern.

"I *do* have feelings," Quin muttered. "I'm not a zombie."

"Who said zombies don't have feelings?"

"Oh my God. I think this conversation is over."

Farrell chuckled. "It's going to be a rough couple of days. Stay safe, Quin. And take care of Katie."

Quin decided to *avoid* Katie as much as possible for the next eight hours. His conversation with Farrell had upended the status quo to an alarming degree. Actually, it wasn't Farrell's fault at all. Quin was waking slowly, like a man who had been in a coma for weeks or months.

For the first time since he was ten years old, skiing was no longer the primary thing on his mind. Nor was he obsessing about his bum knee and how quickly—or not—it was healing.

Even though the storm was still hours away, the ocean was unsettled, the heavens above an angry gray. Clouds scudded across the sky so quickly it was clear that something ominous was just over the horizon.

He grabbed a handful of cashews for lunch and kept at his self-imposed list of chores. Though he didn't have storm shutters, he *did* have several sheets of plywood. They were Farrell's, actually. Picked up during a recent run to a building supply store. Farrell was planning to use them in his new lab. Now Quin conscripted them for a more urgent need.

He balanced them one at a time on a wheelbarrow and moved them around to the front of the house. It didn't take long to realize that he needed Katie's help. *Damn it.* Even if he didn't have a weak knee at the moment, the heavy plywood would have been awkward for one person to carry up the front stairs.

When he texted her, she came and found him right away. "Quin. Is it really going to be that bad?" She assessed his project immediately.

"Farrell says yes. I remembered this plywood. I need you to help me get it up the stairs and then steady it while I hammer the nails. I've already taken the stepladder up to the porch."

Her glare was full-on warrior Katie. "Farrell and Zachary sent me here to keep you from doing something stupid—remember?"

Quin ground his jaw. "I don't call protecting my property stupid."

She crossed her arms. "You are *not* climbing that ladder. *Capisce?*"

He wanted to argue. He really did. But his knee was already aching like hell from everything he had done yesterday and today. "Fine," he grumbled. "*You* can climb the ladder. But it's still going to take both of us to carry each piece of plywood up these stupid stairs."

She kissed his cheek and nuzzled his nose with hers. "The stairs are beautiful. Quit being grumpy."

He didn't have an answer for that. How could he

tell her he'd had an epiphany that morning? And that it seemed like an eternity until they would both be in bed together again?

In the end, it took them half an hour to get all the plywood up to the porch. Katie got a splinter. Quin wrenched his good knee, because he was favoring the one that had had surgery.

They were both breathing hard and drenched with sweat.

He turned to glance at Katie. She was dressed as casually as he was, with her hair caught up in a pony-tail, and long legs that were mostly bare thanks to tiny khaki shorts that made him drool. "Do you even know how to hammer?" he asked.

Katie lifted her nose and sniffed. Disdainfully. "I've hung pictures at your brother's office. Does that count?" She wiped beads of moisture from her fore-head. "Come on. Let's get this done. I want to go back inside and bask in the air-conditioning before we lose power."

The oncoming storm had pushed thick humid air ahead of it. Maine summers were rarely this hot and sticky. The uncomfortable atmosphere was oppres-sive.

Quin set up the ladder. If Katie stood on the next-to-top step, she would be just tall enough to reach the highest part of the window. As much as it galled him to admit it, this was the only way. Aside from his recovering knee, if they reversed positions, he doubted whether Katie would be able to support the heavy piece of plywood long enough for him to get it nailed into place.

He handed her the hammer. "Put the nails in your pocket. I'll steady the ladder. Put a hand on my shoulder if you need to."

Katie climbed the ladder easily. Only now, he was on eye level with her shapely calves. If he looked upward...

He cleared his throat. "You okay up there?"

"Yep. Just tell me what to do."

"I'm going to pick up the first piece of wood. I'll slide it up the side of the house, and you'll have to tell me when it's in a good spot."

"Got it."

Lifting the plywood over his head was no piece of cake. Again, it struck him that his long convalescence had robbed him of his usual level of fitness. The strength of a skier's arms and shoulders was as integral to peak performance as thighs and knees. He needed to get back to the weight room soon.

In the meantime, he and Katie had to manage this somehow. Ignoring the slender legs in his peripheral vision, he inched the wood up the wall, completely covering the window.

"That's good," Katie said.

"Don't worry about messing up the window frame. It can be replaced. If you don't hit the right spot, get another nail and try again."

Fifteen

Katie's entire body ached. She and Quin had been at this for over three hours. Now they were on the last window.

So far, she had smashed her finger twice and had to redo seven crooked nails. The chore was frustrating and difficult.

At last, she climbed down the ladder and groaned. "Please tell me we're done."

Quin collapsed the ladder. "Yeah. No more wood."

"What about the windows on the second-floor porch?"

"We'll just have to hope for the best. If we weren't so exposed here on this bluff, I wouldn't worry. The two big trees at the corner of the house will provide a little protection."

"Then that's it…right? We've done all we can do?"

He ruffled the ends of her hair. "Looks that way."

"Would you like me to fix spaghetti for dinner? Mrs. Peterson left us a container of homemade sauce."

"That's something we can cook on the propane stove if we lose power. What if I grill steaks outside, and you bake some potatoes and do a salad and garlic bread? We might as well have a feast while we can."

"Okay. You want first shower?"

His grin made her stomach flip. "Don't be silly, Kat. I need you to wash my back."

In the end, the shower lasted far longer than was good for the water supply. Once they were done teasing each other with soap and water, they curled up in Quin's bed, made love and napped. If it weren't for the prospect of a tropical storm, it would have been the perfect afternoon.

Katie was the first one to wake up. She slid out of bed, found clean clothes and went to check the weather. Figaro had only now been downgraded from a hurricane to a tropical storm. The images of damage from Cape Cod were sobering. The storm had meandered out to sea at one point and was now headed west. Prepared to make a second landfall between Bar Harbor and the Stone brothers' property.

She shut off the TV, too unsettled to watch any more news. Might as well get the potatoes in the oven. Quin tracked her down in the kitchen. "You hungry?" he asked.

"Getting there." His jaw was shadowed with two

days' growth of beard. He'd slept with damp hair, which now stuck out at weird angles. A plain white cotton T-shirt stretched across his impressive chest. The jeans that rode low on his body exposed tantalizing glimpses of hip bone.

He was the sexiest man she had ever seen.

Katie braced herself against the edge of the counter. "You sure you want to use the grill? It's getting dark outside…way too soon."

"It's the fastest way. Just tell me when you want the steaks ready and how you like yours."

She glanced at the clock. "Thirty minutes from now. Medium well."

Quin nodded. "Got it."

When he wandered away to prepare the grill, Katie began putting together the salad and spreading pieces of frozen bread on a cookie sheet. Suddenly, a gust of wind shook the house. It faded quickly, but she realized they were getting a taste of what was to come.

While she worked, she kept checking the weather app on her iPad. Quin was right. It looked as if the eye of the storm—or what was left of it—would pass almost directly over Stone River. Because of the way the brothers' houses were situated, all three would take a hit

She couldn't deny that she was nervous. Still, with Quin around, she knew they would be okay. She trusted his intuition, and she felt safe when she was with him. Even so, as the wind began to blow with increasing force, her apprehension deepened.

All of the pieces of their *final* dinner came together

right on time. Quin grabbed a platter for the steaks, and moments later brought them in to the table. He slammed the back door and locked it, shutting out the storm. His shirt was spattered with raindrops. He rubbed his hands together, surveying the food. "A condemned man's last meal."

She punched his arm. "Don't say that. We're still going to eat, even with no power."

"True." He held her chair until she was seated. "But it won't be this good. Canned food never is. We'll eat what's in the fridge as fast as we can before it spoils. After that, we'll be roughing it."

"Maybe we won't lose power."

As if on cue, the entire house went dark.

Quin chuckled. "Right on time." He stood and rummaged in a cabinet for candles and matches. Soon, quiet, flickering flames cast a cozy glow. He kissed the top of her head and sat back down. "Isn't this romantic…"

"Don't make fun of romance, Quin. That's a cheap shot." She scanned his face, searching for proof that he was being condescending.

He held up his hands. "I wasn't. I swear. This is nice."

He wasn't wrong. A scrumptious dinner with a handsome man. The rain beating at the windows. It was the perfect script for a rom-com. Except that Katie didn't feel like laughing. She had let herself get in way too deep with this relationship—with this fling that was supposed to be fun and temporary. Now the storm had cut off any escape.

Katie picked at her food. "I'm going to check the weather," she said.

"Do you still have a phone signal?"

She nodded. "One bar. For the moment." She clicked over to radar and showed the screen to Quin. The lopsided red and yellow spiral was almost on top of them.

He cursed beneath his breath. "Look how wide it is."

"And the rainfall totals…"

"Yes. The fact that it still has sustained winds over seventy miles an hour means it's barely below hurricane strength. This house is built to modern codes. We'll just have to hope for the best."

When dinner was done, Katie prowled from room to room, too nervous to sit. Quin settled back in the living room with a book and a candle and those sexy glasses. She loved to read, but she didn't see how he could concentrate with all the racket from outside.

The house actually shook. If this *wasn't* an actual hurricane, she couldn't imagine a Cat 4 or a Cat 5. That would be terrifying. Tropical Storm Figaro was bad enough.

Finally, she grabbed her yoga mat from Quin's bedroom, put it down on the runner in the hallway and ran through a familiar, comfortable sequence of poses. The more she stretched and tried to quiet her mind, the louder the storm became.

Now the wind howled. Like a banshee. It sounded as if every shingle was being ripped from the roof one at a time, though that was probably her imagination.

By this point in her exercise routine, she had typically found her center, her breathing deep and restorative.

Tonight, she was toast. Her yoga teacher would be very disappointed.

Finally, she gave up. Her body was limber and warm, sweaty actually, but her anxiety was out of control. It was the not knowing that was the hardest. How could Quin sit there so calmly? Was this how he prepared for a huge downhill race? Was he so good at focusing his mind that he could shut out the storm entirely?

She poked her head into the room where he sat reading. "I'm going to take another shower."

Quin didn't look up from his book, but he waved a hand to acknowledge that he heard her. She grabbed a change of clothes and closed herself in the bathroom. At this rate, she'd soon be forced to do laundry in the sink. The house was still cool so far. That would change.

The hot, stinging spray on her bare skin actually helped. But when she shut off the shower, immediately the storm was in the room with her. How long did a tropical storm last? Two hours? Four?

She was surprised Quin hadn't suggested sex as a way to pass the time, but he probably realized they wouldn't be able to concentrate. Or at least Katie wouldn't. Men had a knack for shutting out the entire world when it came to sex.

It dawned on her suddenly that she was missing her contacts. She had probably forgotten to unload one of the drawers in the guest bath. In a minute, she would fetch them. But she couldn't resist the urge to join Quin on the sofa. He wrapped an arm around her shoulders and kept reading.

It was a biography. A book about a Swiss skiing legend.

She snuggled closer. "Is it good? The book, I mean."

He gave her a quick glance. "Actually, yes." He shut the book, but kept his finger in as a bookmark. "Are you okay, Katie?"

"Yes. No. I'm rattled."

His lips curled upward in one of those mouthwatering grins that made her stomach wobble. "Farrell always describes you as unflappable."

She snorted. "Your brother has never subjected me to a hurricane."

"Tropical storm. Don't exaggerate."

"ToMAYto, toMAHto."

"You can't blame me for this. I don't control the weather. Are you really scared?"

"Not so much scared as antsy." She shrugged. "It would help if I could take a walk or chop some wood."

His lips twitched. "Chop wood?"

"It's a metaphor. For somebody who reads so much, I'd think you would know about metaphors."

He put the book on the coffee table. "You're getting snippy now. Maybe we need a distraction."

"Oh no," she said, jumping to her feet. "No funny business from Mr. Sexy Stud. I have to make sure this storm is going to leave us."

"So you're tempted, but I have to sublimate my male desires so you can boss around a hurricane?"

"Tropical storm."

He threw back his head and chuckled. She loved making him laugh.

Quin tapped his fingers on the arm of the sofa. Maybe he wasn't as calm as he seemed. "I thought *you* were reading a book in bed last night."

"I was. Can't concentrate on the words right now. Besides, I think I left my little case of contacts upstairs. I wear the disposable dailies. I'm going to run and get them. Be right back."

She was gone before Quin could stop her.

He was probably at least as concerned as Katie, but he knew if he confessed that the storm was more dangerous than he had expected, it would only make matters worse. He didn't like the idea of her being on the second floor without him. The roof might fly off. Who the hell knew?

This was his first tropical storm, too.

Suddenly, a ferocious crash echoed through the house accompanied by a female scream—a Katie scream. He shot down the hall and up the stairs, barely pausing to acknowledge the strain on his new knee.

Up here the storm was even louder. And then he saw the worst part. A huge limb had ripped loose from one of the nearby trees. The wind had hurled it through the window, a projectile that shattered glass and let in sheets of rain and the fury of Figaro.

Katie was kneeling just inside the door of the bedroom, holding her arm. It was too damn dark. He reached for her, crunching through large shards of glass. "Are you hurt?"

He didn't mean to shout, but he was terrified, and he could barely hear his own words over the cacophony of the gale.

She stood up. "I'm bleeding." Her voice wobbled.

Quin ripped off his T-shirt and tried to wrap her injury. Katie jerked backward. "Don't touch me, please. The glass is still in my arm."

Nausea heaved in his belly. "Stay calm, Kat. Let's get you downstairs so I can take a look."

"We have to cover the window," she said. "The water will ruin your floor."

"I don't give a rat's ass about the floor, crazy woman." He started to scoop her up into his arms and then groaned. If he tried to carry her down the stairs, they might both end up dead.

"We're going to walk down slowly," he said, moderating his tone. Yelling at Katie wasn't going to help a thing.

"Okay," she whispered.

It felt like a million hours before they made it to the bottom of the staircase. The only illumination came from the candle he had left burning in the living room.

Katie whimpered, the sound quiet and heartbreaking. He wasn't even sure she knew she was doing it.

On the bottom step, he stopped her. "We need to

take off our shoes. So we don't track broken glass through the house."

She nodded. "Let me hold your shoulder."

Clumsily, she shed her slippers one at a time and stepped onto the floor below. Then it was Quin's turn. His deck shoes were not too bad to toe off. He left both of them on that same step and joined Katie.

"First things first," he said. "Let me get the flashlights. We don't want to drain our phone batteries." He felt like a fool for waiting until now. His only excuse was that Katie had seemed to enjoy the ambience of the candlelight. She'd obviously used her cell phone light when she ran upstairs.

He put her in a living room chair. "Don't move." She was still holding her arm, so he couldn't gauge the extent of her injury. "I'm only going to the kitchen. Won't take but a minute."

Fortunately, he and his brothers were very serious about disaster preparedness. Quin had a stash of matches and flashlights and all sorts of other necessary gear, particularly for winter. Not that the latter was any help at the moment.

He grabbed two sturdy flashlights and went back to Katie. Her head rested against the back of the chair. Her eyes were closed. When he turned on the flashlight and pointed it in her direction, his heart lurched. There was blood everywhere. All down her shirt and onto her pants.

"My God, Kat. Where are you hurt?"

She moved her protective hand. At last, he could see what had happened. When the branch crashed through the window, a piece of shattered glass had embedded itself in Katie's forearm. Blood still oozed slowly. The shard extended outward half an inch.

He'd suffered plenty of injuries over the years. This was far worse. This was *Katie*.

Swallowing the lump in his throat, he sat on the coffee table. "Do you want me to bring the first aid stuff in here, or can you make it to the bathroom?" Her eyes didn't seem quite focused. He worried she was in shock.

She took a deep breath. Tried to smile. Failed. "I can walk," she said. With his help, she stood up slowly. "Is the room supposed to be spinning?" she asked, leaning into him heavily.

"Don't pass out on me, love."

"I won't."

He wouldn't place money on that bet. They made their way to his bedroom. Quin grabbed a small chair with his free hand and dragged it with them to the bathroom. He eased her into a seated position then folded a towel lengthwise. "Rest your head against the edge of the counter if you need to."

"Please don't touch my arm."

Hell, she hated splinters, and this was a splinter on steroids. "We have to clean it, at least," he said quietly, trying to make the tone of his voice as reassuring as possible. "I'll use hydrogen peroxide. It won't hurt at all. Shouldn't even sting." *He hoped*...

Katie sighed. "Okay."

While he rummaged under the sink for a plastic basin and everything else he would need, he snatched a surreptitious glance at Katie's wound. The piece of glass looked obscene. As far as he could tell, the cut was an inch and a half long. Depending on how deep the glass had shoved beneath her skin, she might need stitches.

He set the rectangular bowl across her lap. "Rest your wrist and forearm on the edges of the plastic."

It was clear that she was dubious. It was also clear she was in pain. Her face was dead white, and the furrow between her brows deepened every time she moved. Gingerly, she laid her arm where he had indicated.

Quin uncapped the bottle and removed the protective foil seal. Carefully, he poured a stream of liquid over the cut. Around the edges of the glass, the wound frothed and foamed.

Katie rested her head on the towel, her eyes closed. "That should do it," he said.

Her chin wobbled. "You have to remove the glass, don't you?"

He stroked her hair. "Yes."

Tears rolled down her cheeks. Quiet. Devastating. "I don't think I can do this," she whispered.

Sixteen

Katie felt like such a baby. In her defense, she had never done well with blood.

Quin left her only long enough to return to the bedroom and find another small stool. Now he could sit beside her eye to eye. His gaze was confident and kind. "Do you trust me, Kat?"

She nodded. "Yes."

"I want you to know exactly what's going to happen. No surprises, I promise. When you're ready, I'm going to pull out the shard. Don't move at all, because we can't risk breaking the piece. The wound will start to bleed again, I'm sure. As soon as I finish…" He gulped, looking a little green around the gills himself. "As soon as I finish, I'm going to apply pressure for a few minutes. Then, I have some butterfly bandages that will hold the edges together until we can get you to a doctor."

"Which might be tomorrow or a week from now."

He scowled. "Whatever happens, we'll keep it clean and put antiseptic cream on it."

"I feel like I'm going to barf," she muttered.

Quin stood, found a clean washcloth, wet it and wrapped it around the back of her neck. "Better?" he asked.

She waited a few seconds, breathed shallowly and finally nodded. "I'm okay."

"The longer we wait, the more anxious you're going to be. But I'm not going to pull on it until you're ready. It's your call."

Katie wanted to burrow into a hole and never come out again. The storm still thundered on the roof. The eaves shrieked and groaned. "You could cover the broken window first," she said.

Quin's expression grew stern. "Procrastination is for weak-minded people. You're a warrior, Katie. A woman people depend on. You can do this."

He seemed so sure she was brave. But she wasn't. Not at all. "Can I hold your hand?" she begged. She had started to shake all over. And the nausea returned.

"No. I need both hands free to do this. Either close your eyes or turn your head."

Quin had been through so much physical trauma in his life. He'd been in a terrible car accident. He had endured multiple surgeries. Katie wasn't going to embarrass herself. If he thought she could handle this operation, maybe she could.

She turned over the washcloth on the back of her neck, tucking the cooler side against her skin. "In the old Westerns, they used to give the person a piece of leather to bite down on. Or whiskey to drink."

"Katie." He stared her down, forcing her to gnaw her lip. "Fine," she muttered. "Just do it."

"And you swear you won't move?"

"I'll do my best."

He stood and leaned over her, propping the flashlight at the correct angle with a towel and adjusting the beam. "I can't jerk it, Kat. But I'll be as quick as I can."

"Okay." Her eyes swam with tears. She looked away so he wouldn't see what a wimp she was.

What happened next was not something she ever wanted to repeat. Quin got a firm hold on the ragged edge of the glass and began to pull. *Damn it.* It hurt like hell. She counted to ten and then to fifty.

Suddenly it was over.

"It's out," Quin said. He sat down hard. Her arm gushed blood. Quin grabbed another clean washcloth—maybe she would have to buy him a dozen new ones—and held it against her arm tightly.

Even with the glass gone, the pressure hurt. She rested her forehead against his shoulder. "Thank you," she whispered. He cupped the back of her neck with his free hand and drew her closer. "Don't ever make me go through that again, Kat. Hurting you is harder than anything I've had to do in my life."

"It wasn't so bad."

"Liar."

They sat there in an awkward embrace for fifteen minutes. Finally, he eased the terry cotton aside. A trickle of blood continued, but not the heavy flow from before.

"Do you think you got it all?" she asked.

"I hope so. I'm going to rinse it one more time. Then I'll bandage it."

The hydrogen peroxide bubbled fiercely in the open wound, removing any tiny pieces of glass that remained, she hoped. Afterward, Quin patted her arm dry with a tissue. Next, he applied two butterfly bandages that pulled the edges of the cut together.

Finally, it was done.

He sighed deeply and stood to clean up the mess. "We should go to bed," he said. "Who knows what tomorrow will bring…"

"What about the window?"

His eyes widened. "Hell."

"You forgot?"

"Yes." He shook his head in disbelief. "I'll cover it. Once I have you tucked into bed."

"Oh no," Katie said. "I'm going to sit at the bottom of the stairs and make sure you're okay. I'd go back up there if I could, but my knees are wobbly."

"Join the club," he joked. He held her arm while they walked down the hall. When she was seated, he disappeared briefly and returned with a large blue tarp, sturdy electrical tape and some old rags.

He stepped into his shoes and steadily climbed the stairs. As he made it higher, she could hear glass crunch beneath his feet.

"How bad is it?" she yelled.

"Pretty bad. Maybe we'll install a pool up here."

The fact that he still retained his sense of humor buoyed her flagging spirits. As she listened intently, she heard him curse and mutter as he wrestled the tarp into place.

"Is it working?" she cried.

Quin's voice drifted down the stairs, even over the sound of the rain. "I think so. The windowsills are wet, so the tape doesn't want to stick."

"Don't cut yourself."

"Don't worry. I'm being careful."

At last, the sound of the rain was muffled. Thank God.

Quin came down the stairs, stepping gingerly. "I don't know if it will hold, but I did the best I could for tonight."

He took her hand and pulled her to her feet. "That arm is going to ache pretty badly once the adrenaline wears off. Can you take hydrocodone?"

"As long as I have some food with it. Crackers, maybe?"

"How about a piece of Mrs. Peterson's famous pound cake? I was saving it for a breakfast surprise, but I think we could use a slice right now. With milk? How does that sound?"

"How fast does milk go bad?"

"Not this fast. We might as well drink it tonight."

She perched at the kitchen island while Quin prepared their snack. "I think the wind is not as loud as it was before," she said. "Is that wishful thinking on my part?"

He paused and cocked his head. "Maybe. But the rain will last longer, I think."

Katie swallowed the pain pill and yawned. "Can I help you clean up anything?"

"No. Go get your jammies on. Take this other flashlight. I'll be there in a minute."

After brushing her teeth and taking off her blood-soaked clothes, Katie washed up as best she could. She knew that getting in the shower was not a good idea with her wound still so new.

There was nothing comfy left to wear in her suitcase. Feeling both bold and guilty, she opened one of Quin's drawers and found a clean T-shirt. It fell to her knees and smelled of laundry detergent. She slid it over her head awkwardly. Her arm protested.

Suddenly, crippling exhaustion overtook her. It was all she could do to stumble toward the bed and fold back the covers.

Quin had to turn off Katie's flashlight. She was already asleep. He was so tired he could barely move. The day and night had taken on a surreal quality. After a few quick ablutions in the bathroom, he stripped off his clothes and slid naked beneath the sheets.

Though he was careful not to bump Katie's arm, he wanted to hold her while they slept. He dragged her close and spooned her, inhaling the scent of her hair. He loved her. The realization was no longer shocking.

Now all he wanted to do was get them out of this mess.

Surely, after all they had been through together these last weeks—surely Katie felt the same way. The fact that he still had doubts made his chest tight with uncertainty and dread.

His whole life had been turned upside down since the car accident. But one thing was becoming clear. Losing his skiing prowess had hurt him deeply. Losing Katie would destroy him.

The next morning, Quin faced a quandary. He wanted to stay in bed and cuddle with Katie. But the storm had passed, and he knew he had to assess the damage. He dressed rapidly and left the bedroom, hoping she would sleep longer. It was barely seven.

The sun shone down brightly, with benevolent warmth, as if nothing bad had happened. When Quin stepped out the back door, his spirits sank. As far as the eye could see, the forest was littered and crippled. The beautiful white pines had been most vulnerable, because they were the tallest and their canopies had little protection from surrounding trees.

Inland, it wouldn't have been so bad, but here on the beach even without official hurricane winds, dozens of trees had fallen. The road out, the one to the main highway, was impassable without many hours of chain saw work. Going the mile and a half north to Zachary's place would be no better.

Though Quin couldn't see them from the house, the airstrip and helicopter pad were probably unusable, as well. He and Katie were well and truly stuck.

He decided to fire up the generator. Katie had said she needed to do laundry, and they could eat a big lunch to use up as much of the still-edible food as possible. When he finally went back inside, he found her in the bedroom. She had pulled on a pair of stretchy yoga pants, and if he wasn't mistaken, she was wearing one of his T-shirts. She greeted him with a smile. "The power's back on."

He shook his head. "Sorry to burst your bubble, but it's the generator."

Katie nodded. "Ah. Well, then, I'd better get busy."

"First things first." He took her wrist and reeled her in. The kiss was long and deep and left both of them struggling to breathe. He cleared his throat. "I need to check your arm."

"I think it's okay."

The cut looked raw but not infected. Hopefully, it would stay that way. "Let me know when you're going to shower," he said, "and I'll wrap your arm in plastic. Just today. It's a nasty cut. We need to be careful."

She nodded. "Laundry first. Once I have that going, I'll see about lunch. It will be on the early side."

"No problem. I don't want to run the generator too long, so that works. We'll make it our big meal and snack for dinner."

"How long do you think we'll be here?"

"Honestly? I don't know."

The mundane conversation covered a deep vein of subtext. Quin wanted to tell her he loved her, but because of the storm, he sensed the time was not right.

Not only that, but he was still coming to terms with his feelings. *Love* was a big four-letter word. He had to be sure. Though it was hard to wait, he decided to use this quiet time together to savor the moment. Maybe even formulate a few hazy future plans.

Protecting Katie was his first priority. Quin knew the commentary that was running in *his* head. Katie was less easily understood. She had dealt with the crisis like a champ. But what was she *really* thinking?

For Katie, the day passed slowly. She now had her original suitcase full of clean clothes. At lunch, she and Quin had feasted on spaghetti and salad and the last vestiges of two cartons of ice cream from the now-useless freezer. Afterward, she had insisted on cleaning up the kitchen herself. Quin had plenty to do outside. She knew he was trying to clear the garage and driveway in order to get a vehicle out.

At eleven thirty when the generator shut off, she grimaced. It wouldn't be long until the house heated up again. Though Quin wouldn't like it, she found a broom and climbed the stairs. Sweeping up the glass and tiny bits of leaves and twigs from the smashed window at least made her feel useful.

Once that was done, she used bleach wipes to clean the blood spatters. The place looked like a crime scene. Reliving last night made her feel a little sick. Even so, she and Quin had come through the disaster relatively unscathed.

She was happy to see that the rockers on the porch had survived the storm. The bungee cords had held, but the chairs had taken a beating and would need to be repainted. She wouldn't be here to see that.

Acknowledging the coming break with Quin made her heart hurt worse than her arm. According to the original agreement with the Stone brothers, she had two weeks and change left to fulfill her obligation.

The truth was, though, she and Quin had worked through the backlog of CEO paperwork efficiently. If she left today, Stone River Outdoors would be in good shape.

It was up to her to be smart. Athletes talked about wanting to go out on top. She and Quin were in a better place than they had ever been. He was affectionate and caring. And he had changed. He had let her in, let her get close.

But his father's words still haunted Katie. Part of her still believed them. Quin wasn't the kind of guy who settled down to marriage, even though he cared deeply about her. Maybe more than he had cared about any other woman.

What hurt so badly was knowing he might never reconcile himself to the huge loss he had suffered. It was one thing for Quin to decide to hang up his skis at a particular age. That wasn't what happened, though. He had been robbed of his future. Was he using Katie to assuage his pain and loss?

In the midst of her soul-searching, Quin came and found her. "I've got the Jeep out," he said. "And cleared the driveway. I'm going to see how far I can get toward the airstrip. The chain saw is gas powered. I'll try to drag smaller trees out of the way. The bigger ones I can cut into pieces. If we can get a wide enough space cleared off for the chopper, one of my brothers will find a way to help us. You want to ride along?"

"Definitely. It will go faster with two."

He frowned. "You're hurt. You'll stay in the Jeep."

"No, I won't." she said firmly. "I have one good arm. I'll do what I can to help."

Quin scowled. "I have never met a more stubborn woman."

"Pot. Kettle. So it's okay for you to run the show, but I'm not supposed to get involved? Think again, Quin. I'm going with you."

Seventeen

Quin wiped sweat from his eyes and glared up at the sun. You'd think after a hell of a storm that Mother Nature would give them a break. Today's heat was likely record-breaking.

Katie never once complained. Their progress was painfully slow. They drove several hundred yards. Stopped. Dragged a tree out of the road. Back in the Jeep. Maybe only a few hundred feet the second time. Then another tree. Every third or fourth one had to be cut up because it was too heavy.

By five o'clock they had to call it quits.

Katie chewed her lip, her hair bedraggled and sticking to her forehead, big brown eyes wide with worry. "But what if they fly up here and can't land, because we didn't get finished?"

"Farrell and Zachary probably have plenty to do in Portland at the moment. They both know I have supplies. If phone and power haven't been restored by the weekend, *then* they might try to come north. We have time."

They drove back to the house and took turns in the shower. Again, Katie didn't complain. The water felt shockingly cold. Quin's fingernails were blue by the time he was done.

It felt good to be clean and dry, at least.

He fired up the small propane stove. They dined on baked beans and canned ham. It wasn't much, but it did the job. They still had enough pound cake for dessert.

Katie took her dishes to the sink and, on the way back, leaned over his shoulder from behind and nuzzled his neck. "Do you like card games? I'm pretty good."

He stood and scooped her up for a hard kiss. "Strip poker?" he asked hopefully.

She grinned. "I was thinking rummy."

"Bor-ing."

Quin happened to be pretty good at card games himself. In college, he'd played poker for money and kicks. Katie, on the other hand was a shark. With her innocent face, gorgeous eyes and distracting breasts, she beat him the first game.

His competitive instincts kicked in. "Rematch," he said, giving her his best intimidating stare.

She shrugged. "As long as you don't mind being humiliated. Again."

This time, he tried. He really did. The outcome was the same.

After four straight losses, he held up his hands in surrender. "I give up. Katie Duncan is queen bee of the rummy world."

"I warned you." Her amused smile caught something in his chest and twisted it. He still didn't know why she'd walked away from their relationship two years ago. She had insisted that this six-week stint in the Maine woods was strictly temporary. And truth be told, the first three weeks were a waste, because they hadn't been intimate. Had anything happened between them in the meantime to change her mind?

God, he hoped so. He loved her. That wasn't going to change. But was he any better equipped to be the man she wanted? He thought he could be. Katie was more real to him now. Not simply a woman to satisfy a momentary physical craving.

Every day they spent together revealed new facets of her personality. Things he'd been blind to before. And the more he knew about her, the more deeply he fell under her spell.

Whatever it took, however long he had to wait, he would make her understand. The stakes were too high to give up.

"I want to make love to you," he blurted out.

Her cheeks turned pink. Or at least he thought they did. Beyond the windows, the light was beginning to fade. "It's barely eight o'clock," she said, sounding both scandalized and interested.

He kissed the inside of her wrist. "We're both beat. Who cares what we do, Katie? The night is ours."

Half an hour later, Katie let him drag her toward the bedroom.

The way she wanted him was not entirely sane. She had lived by intellect her entire life. Until now. With Quin, all she wanted to do was wallow in her need for him, feel deeply and drown in the incredible pleasure he gave her.

Their evenings were governed by candlelight after the storm. It was a dangerous glow. Subtly arousing. Endlessly romantic.

They undressed in tandem and met in the center of the mattress. *I love you, Quin.* The words trembled on her lips. How would he react if she gave voice to them?

Never once had he given any indication that he felt anything deeper than lust. Tonight was the first time he had said "make love" instead of "have sex." Was the change in wording significant, or was she simply another pitiful woman desperate to believe?

They touched each other endlessly, drunk on the solitude and their gratitude for being alive. She was sleepy and her arm ached, and still she wanted him. When he slid inside her, it was like coming home after a long, hard journey. Quin promised protection and comfort and peace.

But more than that, enchanting sexual pleasure.

Her orgasm built to a warm, honeyed peak that

198 AFTER HOURS SEDUCTION

flowed into deep relaxation. She heard and felt Quin
find his own release.

They fell asleep instantly in a tangle of arms and legs.

The following morning, it rained. Hard. A steady
deluge punctuated by lightning and thunder. They
hadn't seen it coming, because they no longer had
the luxury of forecasts and radar.

"We can't go out in this," Katie said. "It isn't safe."

Quin had smudges beneath his eyes. His jaw tightened. "I know."

He was like a caged tiger today. Sulky and vibrating with ill-concealed frustration.

She knew his bad mood had nothing to do with her,
or at least she didn't think so, but telling him to chill
out wouldn't help. Quin was a man who hated inac-
tion. This waiting for the storm to be over was hard
on both of them. She decided it was best to keep her
distance. "I'll do some more cleaning upstairs. Just
to keep busy. How about you?"

He drummed his fingers on the table. "I suppose
I could go through my father's papers out in the garage. When the house was sold after he died, all the
contents were listed and offloaded in an estate sale.
My brothers boxed up the contents of four filing cabi-
nets from Dad's office and sent them here for me
to deal with. I assume the bulk of it is garbage. But
there will be stuff pertaining to SRO that we should
probably keep."

"I doubt I'd be any help with that."

"Probably not."

"Peanut butter sandwiches at noon?" Mrs. Peterson had left two fresh loaves of bread.

Quin nodded. "Sure." Then he paused. "I don't need you to look after my house, Kat. I can pay for a cleanup crew when the time comes."

"I know. But I can't go outside and climb down to the beach. Even if I wanted to walk in the woods, the trails are a mess. I have to do *something*, or I'll go crazy."

Finally, he gave her a reluctant grin. As if he had been enjoying his bad mood. "You and me both. But please be careful."

"I will. You, too."

"There's nothing dangerous in the garage."

"I hope not. I've had enough shocks for one week." She kissed his cheek. "See you at lunch."

Quin hated paperwork more than just about anything. Which was why he'd been putting off this unwelcome chore. But he needed something to occupy his thoughts. Some kind of distraction. Thinking about how to tell Katie he loved her and wondering about the fallout afterward was driving him nuts.

Months ago, Farrell had purchased an oversize shredding bin on wheels, but the electricity was out, so the shredder was useless. Quin found two empty boxes and set them beside a folding lawn chair.

His plan was to toss unimportant stuff in one box and shred it in the future. If he came across anything that seemed valuable, those pages would go in box number two. He and Farrell and Zachary could go through those items together. At a later date.

He grabbed a couple of water bottles and settled in for his boring morning. As he suspected, most of the reams of file folders were filled with minutiae. His father had saved everything.

Quin found a receipt for dry cleaning from 1991. And that was only the tip of the iceberg.

When he finished the first box, he stood and stretched the kinks out of his back, downing half a bottle of water at the same time. It was gratifying to realize that his knee was no worse for the wear after all he had put it through in the last few days.

Slow healing was hard to track. Today, though, it was clear to him that he was definitely better. Perhaps at some visceral level he had been afraid his knee would never again be reliable. But that wasn't so. He was on the mend for sure this time. Third surgery a charm.

As much as it galled him to admit it, his brothers and the doctor had been right. His leg as a whole had needed time to recover. Six weeks of taking it easy was a small price to pay for the prospect of normalcy.

And then there was Katie. What was he going to do about Katie?

Sighing deeply, he forced himself to sit down and get back to work.

The second box didn't have a million slips of paper like the first one. Here, he found his father's personal checkbook registers and bank statements. Even with the advent of online everything, his dad had preferred the mental security of keeping everything under lock and key.

These were his personal transactions. Political contributions. Purchases large and small. Cars. Bespoke suits. Gold cuff links.

Quin couldn't imagine he would find anything relevant to the workings of Stone River Outdoors, but he continued to flip through the entries just in case. One name caught his eye.

Caught his eye and made his stomach clench.

Katie Duncan. $100,000.

In his father's distinctive handwriting. The entry was unmistakable, as was the date. The check had been written two years ago. In the same month Katie broke up with him.

His brain literally went numb. Thoughts floated in and out of his head, but nothing stuck. The feelings of hurt and disbelief crushed him as he tried to think back to that time. He and Katie had been arguing about money. As always. Katie had been about to drain her personal savings account in order to send her sister's loser boyfriend to rehab.

Quin had been vehemently opposed to the idea and furious that Katie's sister would take advantage of her that way. No drug addict was ever successfully rehabilitated unless the person in question *wanted* to change.

Katie had stood her ground. She told him he didn't know what it was like to have a dysfunctional family. She told him her choices were her own.

And a very short time later, she had ended their relationship.

She had never *asked* Quin for the money. Maybe she had been hoping he would offer. Hell, no. Not in that situation.

So what had Katie done? Gone to Quin's father and brazenly requested a loan? Surely the old man hadn't simply handed over the money.

Everyone at Stone River Outdoors loved Katie, so it was conceivable that his father might have had a soft spot for her. But an outright gift of that magnitude, no way. The old man was a tightfisted bastard. Not even for a pretty girl would he part with his hard-earned dollars.

But clearly, he had.

Quin felt hollow inside. Gutted. By all accounts, Katie had never wanted Quin's money. But maybe he had been so emotionally disconnected he hadn't recognized her need for help. Had she been in such a bad spot that Quin himself had forced her to borrow money from his father rather than ask her lover?

If he'd been that clueless, it was no wonder she broke up with him.

Even now, a tiny part of him felt betrayed. She had left him once before without a satisfactory explanation.

Had he earned her trust this time around? Did *he* trust *her*?

He stood and kicked the box with his good leg. The pain in his toes stoked his misery. Gripping the ledger, white-knuckled, he stalked into the house.

* * *

Katie hummed as she worked. It felt good to stretch her muscles and do something useful. She was careful not to bang her arm. After breakfast, Quin had cleaned the cut and put new butterfly strips on the ugly gash. The margins of the wound were a healthy pink. He had mentioned plastic surgery, but that seemed unnecessary.

She had run out of paper towels, so she scooted down the now-immaculate stairs to get more supplies from the kitchen. Just as she reached the foyer, Quin confronted her, his face dark, his expression frightening.

He stuck out his arm, waving some kind of diary in her face. "Would you like to explain this to me?"

Katie had never seen him so angry. She took a step backward. "I don't know. What is it?"

"Maybe you've never seen this particular ledger, but you sure as hell will remember this entry."

She took the leather-bound book from him, because she had no other choice.

Quin stabbed a finger at the left-hand page. "Recognize anything?"

She glanced down. There in neat printing was her name. And an amount. Her heart sank. "I was hoping you would never have to see this. I'm so sorry, Quin."

He gazed at her. His face went dead white. "You're not denying it?"

"How can I?" she asked, confused. "He wrote that check. I didn't want you to find out. I knew it would hurt you So I kept the secret."

Quin scraped a hand through his hair, his eyes filled with some strong emotion. He was clearly distraught. "Why wouldn't you ask *me* for the money? Why ask my father? Did you think so little of me that you believed I wouldn't help you when you needed it?"

He stopped, stared, and gave her a stricken look. "And I suppose you thought when he died, you were off the hook. That you wouldn't have to pay the money back, because it was a *secret*."

In one blinding instant, Katie realized that he had misunderstood. Her legs trembled. Her stomach clenched and heaved. "Wait," she said. "You actually think I took money from your father without telling you?"

Her heart shattered, leaving fragments far more painful than the one that had lodged in her arm. She was too shocked to defend herself.

"Don't try to spin this, Katie. It's all out in the open now."

Before she could answer his sickening accusation, thunderous knocking sounded at the front door. Suddenly, Farrell and Zachary burst in, their faces painted in distress.

Quin's jaw dropped. "How did you get here? We haven't even been able to clear the helipad yet."

Both brothers enveloped him in a bear hug. Then they shook Katie's hand. "We were worried sick about both of you," Farrell said, "so I chartered a boat. Half the roads in the state are impassable. God knows how long it will be until basic utilities are restored this far north. We've come to take you back to Portland."

Zach zeroed in on Katie's bandaged arm. "Are you okay?"

She nodded. "I'm fine. Why don't all of you go to the kitchen and grab a sandwich. I'll pack my things. Honestly, I can't wait to get out of here."

Quin shot her a dark look as the three brothers disappeared down the hall. As if he was telling her, *this isn't over yet.*

In a matter of minutes, she had removed every trace of her presence from Quin's bedroom. She didn't want his brothers to know she and Quin had been sleeping together. She dragged it all upstairs so she could organize and pack for the trip home.

Which meant that half an hour later, the two older Stone brothers watched her descend the stairs from the guest suite as if she had been staying there all along. Zach met her halfway. "Here. Let me help you with those bags."

"Where's the boat?" she asked, feeling dead inside. That Quin could think she would go behind his back and betray him meant he still had no clue who she was. They hadn't connected at all. Not really. Not if Quin had jumped to such an appalling conclusion.

Farrell answered. "The captain is anchored just offshore. No clearance for a big vessel on Quin's tiny, rocky beach. We waded in, but one of us will help you."

Eighteen

Quin seethed during the long trip back to Portland. The rain stopped. The sun came out. Nothing could improve his mood. He told himself he was furious, but even he recognized his own lie. He was hurt. Slashed to the bone.

When Katie had ended the relationship two years ago, he had imagined any number of reasons why she had walked away from some of the best sex of his life. Maybe she hadn't felt the same way. Maybe she was squeamish about the work connection.

Never in a million years had he imagined anything like this.

He stayed in the front cabin of the boat, debriefing with his brothers. Katie sat out in the sunshine, her face turned toward the horizon. She hadn't spoken a word to him or vice versa since Farrell and Zachary arrived.

Surely his brothers had noticed the tension. If they had, neither of them commented. The trip back to Portland took forever. When they docked, a car was waiting for them.

"We'll drop Katie first," Farrell said. "Then the three of us can look over some damage reports from the warehouse and the office."

Twenty minutes later Katie said a general goodbye to the occupants of the car. Zach helped her with her bags. Katie looked at Farrell. "You'll let me know if you need me at the office before it opens?"

"I will," Farrell said.

Then she was gone.

Quin's chest was hollow.

Farrell had booked a reservation at one of their favorite seafood restaurants that had fortunately sustained only minimal damage. Quin ordered his usual crab cake meal, but tasted none of it. The three men sketched out a plan for repairs and the inevitable shipping backlogs. Finally, after an hour and a half, Farrell frowned at him. "You want to tell us what the hell is going on between you and Katie?"

Quin swallowed hard, feeling as if his dinner was in danger of coming back up. "I found out this morning that two years ago she took a hundred grand from Dad. A loan to send her sister's drug-addicted boyfriend to rehab. Since Dad died, I'm pretty sure she hasn't paid it back."

Farrell and Zach stared at him, dumbstruck. Then

Farrell shook his head. "Nope," he said firmly. "That's impossible. I know Katie. She would be far too proud to accept help like that, even if it *was* for someone else. You've got it wrong, Quin. Dead wrong."

Quin explained about the boxes of papers, and the checking information he had found, and the entry with Katie's name. "I showed her the ledger," he said. "She didn't deny it. Didn't even pretend to be surprised. She said she had kept it a secret, because she knew it would hurt me."

"I'm lost," Zach said.

Farrell patted his hand. "Quin and Katie had a hot and heavy affair two years ago. Kept it under wraps. She broke it off. Try to keep up."

Zach shot him a rude gesture. "I still don't get it, Quin. If you and Katie were an item, why wouldn't she borrow the money from you?"

"That's just it," Quin said. "The thing we argued about the most was money. She always wanted to prop up various people in her family who—as far as I could tell—were all leeches. But she should have known I would help her if she had only asked."

Farrell ordered another round of beers. When the waitress nodded and disappeared, he drummed his fingers on the table. "So Katie never actually *asked you* for the money two years ago?"

"No," Quin said. "She told me she was going to clean out a chunk of her savings. I told her that would be stupid and naive."

"You always did have a way with the ladies," Zach said ruefully.

Farrell was like a dog with a bone. "None of this makes sense. If she was going to use her own money, why would she have gone to Dad, a man she barely knew?"

The pain in Quin's chest began to radiate throughout his body. Maybe he was having a heart attack. "The irony is I was crazy about her. I would have given her the moon if she had asked. Instead, she didn't trust me enough to help her. She told me I was selfish. Then she broke up with me and went behind my back to our father."

This time Zach was the one shaking his head. "That's ridiculous, Quin. Dad was a rat bastard half the time. I can't imagine anyone getting money from him, especially not a woman like Katie. He would have chewed her to pieces."

"Then how do you explain him writing a hundred-thousand-dollar check to my ex-girlfriend? A check she knew about. She said so to my face."

The silence grew. Three men trying to find the answer to an unsolvable equation.

Suddenly, Farrell cursed. "Sasha…"

Quin and Zach stared at him blankly.

Zach leaned forward. "Gonna need more than that buddy."

Quin was too torn up to comment.

Farrell banged his fist on the table. "Think how Dad treated Sasha all those years. Belittling her. Chipping away at her confidence. Trying to keep us apart. What if Dad found out about Quin and Katie's affair somehow and offered her a hundred grand to break up with him? And what if she took the money, not for herself, but because the loser boyfriend needed rehab?"

Quin drained half his beer. "Does that make it any more palatable? She *lied* to me," he muttered. His head ached as if a railroad spike was drilling deep.

Zachary, the financial wunderkind who kept SRO in the black, waved a hand, an arrested look on his face. "What if you're half right, Farrell? What if Dad did exactly what you said? But what if Katie never accepted the money?" He speared Quin with an exasperated glance. "Do you have any proof the check was cashed?"

Quin felt queasy. "No."

Zach pulled out his phone. "Dad hated online banking, so I kept up with it for him. With probate dragging on, I haven't closed that account. What month did you say it was?"

"April." Quin's lips were numb now.

The three of them fell silent as Zach dug into the past. At last, he shot Quin and Farrell a triumphant grin. "I found it. The check never cleared. The money is still there."

Quin sucked in a painful breath. "So, Katie…"

Farrell's sympathetic gaze was almost more than Quin could bear. "Katie was protecting you," Farrell said.

Zachary nodded. "She didn't want you to know what a terrible thing your father, *our* father, had done."

"But she broke up with me anyway. Why?"

Farrell shrugged. "I suppose you'll have to ask her that yourself."

Zach nodded. "If she ever speaks to you again."

* * *

Katie had been scared during the tropical storm. But Quin had been with her.

Now she was physically safe, but her heart was breaking.

How could he believe she would take money from his father and not tell him?

All she had ever wanted was for Quin to understand what motivated her, but even now, he couldn't see the truth. She needed him to love her. To trust her. To let her into his heart. Instead, he had immediately jumped to the worst possible conclusion. Katie had thought they were beginning to build something more than a sexual relationship. Quin had gradually let her in to his head and his heart—or so she had thought.

Maybe he was right about her all along. She was too naive and too trusting. Glass half-full. Rosy-colored spectacles. Pollyanna. Pick your cliché.

Quin had been so tender with her, so caring. She had begun to believe, however stupidly, that the two of them might have a chance after all.

For a long time now, she'd thought that money would ultimately keep them apart. Her lack of it and his embarrassingly large surfeit.

In the end, money had turned out to be a peripheral, a tiny bump in the road. The real problem was that Quin didn't know her at all. And apparently, his tendency to keep his thoughts and feelings under wraps had made her blind to his arrogance and pride.

She could have pulled the covers over her head and wallowed in her misery. But there were people in Portland who had *actual* life-and-death problems. No place to live. No food. No water.

Katie threw herself into the recovery effort, shoving her own pain and loss into a dark place in her soul. She helped serve hot meals. She read to children at an evacuation shelter. She made sure her family and friends were okay. And when Farrell called two days after their return from northern Maine, Katie met her boss at the office to help him and a team of tech geeks get the phone lines and internet up and running again.

She had braced for an encounter with Quin, but he was nowhere in sight. Probably on a plane over the Atlantic looking for a high, snowcapped mountain in Europe where he could risk life and limb. Again.

During the daylight hours she kept herself so busy she could barely *think* about Quin. But at night, in bed, her heart ached so badly she wanted to run far away from Portland. From any reminder of what she had found and lost. Love. At least on her side.

Sleeping alone after being with Quin night after night was so lonely and so terrifyingly empty, she cried until there were no more tears. Curled up with her pillow and her heartbreak, she pondered her future bleakly.

How could she stay at Stone River Outdoors?

Quin had faced many tight races in his life, but none as critical as the one to win Katie's forgiveness. He'd done some painful soul-searching. What he realized was that there was precious little chance she *would* forgive him. Even so, he had to make his apology. And he had to make her understand that none of this was her fault.

He'd been the ass. The betrayer. The recklessly bad judge of character and motive. Even now, when he thought about that terrible morning just before his brothers showed up, his stomach tightened with nausea. Remembering Katie's face... God, she had looked as if he had struck her.

Now here he stood, ten days later, on Katie's front porch. Farrell had assured him she was home.

Quin had brought neither candy nor flowers nor even jewelry. Katie Duncan would not be swayed by empty gestures.

If he had come here too soon, there would have been no opportunity for him to cope with what he was feeling. To understand what he wanted. To make a plan for the future. So he had bided his time, examined his black heart and finally understood.

The important thing here was to make sure Katie heard his apology and recognized that it was true and sincere.

She deserved that much at least.

When he rang the doorbell, his hand was shaking.

He honestly hadn't expected her to answer. The door had a peephole. She had to know it was him.

But the door swung inward, and there she was.

Her gaze swept him from head to toe. "You look terrible," she said. No inflection at all in her voice.

"You don't, Kat. You look gorgeous."

It was true. Her casual shorts and Caribbean-print

halter top framed her beauty in a whimsical summer theme. She was barefoot, blond hair loose and tousled.

When the nickname slipped out, she flinched. "Why are you here, Quin? Farrell said you arranged to have my car returned. I asked him to thank you."

"He did." Still she made no move to let him in to her home. "Katie…" His throat tightened. "I know there's no excuse for what I did, but you have to know how sorry I am."

She was stone-faced. "What exactly did you do Quin? Other than accuse the woman you were sleeping with of being a cheat and a liar and a user?"

When her voice broke on the last word, it was like a knife to his heart. "I won't rationalize my behavior. It was indefensible. But when you stood there so calmly and said you knew about the check, I went a little crazy."

"Yes, you did."

"I brought you this," he said desperately, holding out his hand.

She stared at the manila envelope. "Is it an arrest warrant?"

Her sarcasm was no more than he deserved. "Open the envelope. It's for you."

She looked at her neighbor's house where interested eyes were watching. "Oh, for heaven's sake. Come in. But don't get comfortable."

Quin eased past her and staked out a spot near the doorway to the kitchen. He shoved his hands in his pockets.

Katie sank into a chair and opened the envelope,

extracting the contents slowly. After a few moments, she looked up at him with a frown. "What is this?"

He inhaled sharply, feeling like a fool. "I bought you a piano. It's being delivered tomorrow. The phone numbers are for two women here in Portland who give lessons to adults."

Katie shook her head slowly. Having Quin here in her house was painful and unsettling. Day after day she had worked to forget him. It was a stupid game she played. The aggravating man was imprinted on every cell in her body.

"I don't understand," she said.

His blue-eyed gaze seemed haunted, almost as badly bereft as the broken man she had met in northern Maine, the man who had lost everything that mattered to him.

Quin shrugged. "It's part of my apology. I don't know why you left me two years ago, and I know I've screwed things up royally this time. I love you, Katie. That's all."

The blood rushed to her head. "You love me?"

"I should have told you sooner, but I was waiting until after the storm. I wanted to take you to the Riviera or the Caribbean and propose with some big romantic gesture."

"Propose?" Her voice squeaked.

"Then I realized you don't like all the fuss. But before I could come up with plan B, everything went to hell, and it was too late."

She shuddered. "You were so angry, Quin. At me. You can't imagine how that made me feel."

He bowed his head, his posture dejected. "I know. I saw your face." He squared his shoulders. "I think I was afraid," he said simply, his gaze begging her to understand.

She frowned. "Afraid? Quinten Stone is not afraid of anything."

"Not true." He shrugged. "You left me two years ago with no real explanation. When I saw that check my father wrote, I was afraid you didn't trust me to take care of you. That you thought I was so selfish and shallow I wouldn't do everything in my power to help you."

"I don't understand why you're here now," she said softly. Faint sparkles of hope tried to ignite in her heart, but he had hurt her so badly. "What about your other mistress? What about skiing?"

His head came up. Now his eyes were clear. "I've made my peace with it, Kat. No more competing. That's in my past. I've talked to some people about opening a ski school next winter. Nurturing new talent. But whatever happens, skiing is never again going to come between me and the people I love."

"I see," she said softly, her brain spinning, trying to wrap her head around what he was saying.

Finally, Quin moved closer. Determination carved his features in sharp angles. "I'll say it again, because you probably don't believe me. *I love you, Katie Duncan.*" He didn't wait for her to respond. "So I tried to think of a way to make you understand how sorry I am for what happened. I remembered that day at the museum. And the Renoir, *Two Young Girls at the Piano*. And I remembered how you let me in to your bed that night." He paused and swallowed, the muscles working in his throat. "I would never ski another minute in my life if I could have you back."

She laid the envelope aside. "Do you know why I broke up with you two years ago?"

He winced. "I'm guessing my father made you feel like shit. Chased you away. Told you believable lies."

"No." She stood and went to him, face-to-face, toe-to-toe. "Your father had nothing to do with it. I had already decided to go before he spoke to me."

Quin paled. "So it was my fault all along. Something *I* did. Not my father."

Katie put her hand on his cheek, shaking her head. "You didn't *do* anything. That was the problem. I wanted you to be someone you weren't. I wanted a man who was open and self-aware. The problem was, I didn't know how to ask for what I wanted, and the future seemed hopeless."

"So you gave up on us." The words could have been heated, but his voice was low and steady.

She shrugged helplessly. "We had nothing in common, Quin. Recently, I decided we were in a better place now, but the fact that you believed I would take a large sum of money from your father and not tell you makes me wonder. How could it possibly work?"

He captured her hand with his, pressing her fingertips to his stubbly jaw. His skin was warm. "That's where you're wrong, Kat. We have *everything* in common. Every beat of your heart is mine. When you breathe, I breathe. I can't imagine my life without you in it." He stopped. Released her. Stepped back, as if he couldn't bear to touch her. "Do you love me, Kat?"

She was breaking apart inside, tumbled about by every lie she had told herself. "Yes." Tears she couldn't hold at bay spilled over. She hated feeling so emotional.

But Quin's gaze was suspiciously wet, as well. "Then I'll take that for now. Until you're sure. You'll see, my love. You're everything I need. And if you'll forgive me for my monumental stupidity and cruelty, I'll spend the rest of my life proving to you that we fit together well. As perfectly as two fragments of leaded glass in a Tiffany masterpiece. No one else will do for me, Kat. It's that simple. If you won't have me, I'll be a lonely bachelor."

Joy burst through the long hours and days of grief. "Don't overplay your hand." She threw herself at him and wrapped her arms around his neck, absorbing his strength and heat. "I do adore you," she whispered. "Say it again."

He found her lips with his, kissed her slow and deep, reduced her to mush. "I love you, my dearest Kat," he said, his words unsteady. "And just so you know, I'm going to buy you the biggest, gaudiest diamond I can find and make you wear it every day so the whole world will know you're my woman."

She rested her cheek against his firm, broad chest, inhaling the scent of him, soaking in the happiness that was almost too much to bear. "I think I can live with that, Quentin Stone. Now, if you aren't in too much of a hurry, I'd like to show you my new bed. The headboard is rated for restless sleepers."

He chuckled, his eyes bright. "Sounds like a challenge to me…"

* * * * *

Widower Farrell Stone is content with his life—
even if he'll never let himself love a woman again.
But then in walks his new housekeeper, Ivy Danby.
Will he keep his feelings locked away?
Find out in the next book in the
Men of Stone River trilogy,

Upstairs Downstairs Temptation

Available June 2020!

**WE HOPE YOU ENJOYED
THIS BOOK FROM**

◆ HARLEQUIN
DESIRE

*Luxury, scandal, desire—welcome to
the lives of the American elite.*

Be transported to the worlds of oil barons, family dynasties,
moguls and celebrities. Get ready for juicy plot twists,
delicious sensuality and intriguing scandal.

6 NEW BOOKS AVAILABLE EVERY MONTH!

HDHALO2020

COMING NEXT MONTH FROM

DESIRE

Available June 2, 2020

#2737 THE PRICE OF PASSION
Texas Cattleman's Club: Rags to Riches • by Maureen Child
Rancher Camden Guthrie is back in Royal, Texas, looking to rebuild his life as a member of the Texas Cattleman's Club. The one person who can help him? Beth Wingate, his ex. Their reunion is red-hot, but startling revelations threaten their future.

#2738 FORBIDDEN LUST
Dynasties: Seven Sins • by Karen Booth
Allison Randall has long desired playboy Zane Patterson. The problem? He's her brother's best friend, and Zane won't betray that bond, no matter how much he wants her. Stranded in paradise, sparks fly, but Allison has a secret that could tear them apart...

#2739 UPSTAIRS DOWNSTAIRS TEMPTATION
The Men of Stone River • by Janice Maynard
Working in an isolated mansion, wealthy widower Farrell Stone needs a live-in housekeeper. Ivy Danby is desperate for a job to support her baby. Their simmering attraction for one another is evident, but are their differences too steep a hurdle to create a future together?

#2740 HOT NASHVILLE NIGHTS
Daughters of Country • by Sheri WhiteFeather
Brooding songwriter Spencer Riggs is ready to reinvent himself. His ex, Alice McKenzie, is the perfect stylist for the job. Years after their wild and passionate romance, Alice finally has her life on track, but will their sizzling attraction burn them both again?

#2741 SCANDALOUS ENGAGEMENT
Lockwood Lightning • by Jules Bennett
To protect her from a relentless ex, restauranteur Reese Conrad proposes to his best friend, Josie Coleman. But their fake engagement reveals real feelings, and Josie sees Reese in a whole new way. And just as things heat up, a shocking revelation changes everything!

#2742 BACK IN HIS EX'S BED
Murphy International • by Joss Wood
Art historian Finn Murphy has a wild, impulsive side. It's what his ex-wife, Beah Jenkinson, found so attractive—and what burned down their white-hot marriage. Now, reunited to plan a friend's wedding, the chemistry is still there... and so are the problems that broke them apart.

YOU CAN FIND MORE INFORMATION ON UPCOMING HARLEQUIN TITLES, FREE EXCERPTS AND MORE AT HARLEQUIN.COM.

HDCNM0520

SPECIAL EXCERPT FROM

⬢ HARLEQUIN
DESIRE

*To protect her from a relentless ex, restaurateur Reese
Conrad proposes to his best friend, Josie Coleman.
But their fake engagement reveals real feelings, and
Josie sees Reese in a whole new way. And just as things
heat up, a shocking revelation changes everything!*

Read on for a sneak peek at
Scandalous Engagement
by USA TODAY *bestselling author Jules Bennett.*

"What's that smile for?" he asked.

She circled the island and placed a hand over his heart. "You're
just remarkable. I mean, I've always known, but lately you're just
proving yourself more and more."

He released the wine bottle and covered her hand with his...and
that's when she remembered the kiss. She shouldn't have touched
him—she should've kept her distance because there was that look
in his eyes again. Where had this come from? When did he start
looking at her like he wanted to rip her clothes off and have his
naughty way with her?

"We need to talk about it," he murmured.

It. As if saying the word *kiss* would somehow make this situation
weirder. And as if she hadn't thought of anything else since *it* had
happened.

"Nothing to talk about," she told him, trying to ignore the warmth
and strength between his hand and his chest.

"You can't say you weren't affected."

"I didn't say that."

He tipped his head, somehow making that penetrating stare even
more potent. "It felt like more than a friend kiss."

Way to state the obvious.

"And more than just a practice," he added.

Josie's heart kicked up. They were too close, talking about things that were too intimate. No matter what she felt, what she thought she wanted, this wasn't right. She couldn't ache for her best friend in such a physical way. If that kiss changed things, she couldn't imagine how anything more would affect this relationship.

"We can't go there again," she told him. "I mean, you're a good kisser—"

"Good? That kiss was a hell of a lot better than just good."

She smiled. "Fine. It was pretty incredible. Still, we can't get caught up in this whole fake-engagement thing and lose sight of who we really are."

His free hand came up and brushed her hair away from her face. "I haven't lost sight of anything. And I'm well aware of who we are…and what I want."

Why did that sound so menacing in the most delicious of ways? Why was her body tingling so much from such simple touches when she'd firmly told herself to not get carried away?

Wait. Was he leaning in closer?

"Reese, what are you doing?" she whispered.

"Testing a theory."

His mouth grazed hers like a feather. Her knees literally weakened as she leaned against him for support. Reese continued to hold her hand against his chest, but he wrapped the other arm around her waist, urging her closer.

There was no denying the sizzle or spark or whatever the hell was vibrating between them. She'd always thought those cheesy expressions were so silly, but there was no perfect way to describe such an experience.

And kissing her best friend was quite an experience…

Don't miss what happens next in…
Scandalous Engagement
by USA TODAY *bestselling author Jules Bennett.*

Available June 2020 wherever
Harlequin Desire books and ebooks are sold.

Harlequin.com

Copyright © 2020 by Jules Bennett

HDEXP0520

Get 4 FREE REWARDS!

We'll send you 2 FREE Books
<u>plus</u> 2 FREE Mystery Gifts.

Harlequin Desire® books transport you to the world of the American elite with juicy plot twists, delicious sensuality and intriguing scandal.

YES! Please send me 2 FREE Harlequin Desire novels and my 2 FREE gifts (gifts are worth about $10 retail). After receiving them, if I don't wish to receive any more books, I can return the shipping statement marked "cancel." If I don't cancel, I will receive 6 brand-new novels every month and be billed just $4.55 per book in the U.S. or $5.24 per book in Canada. That's a savings of at least 13% off the cover price! It's quite a bargain! Shipping and handling is just 50¢ per book in the U.S. and $1.25 per book in Canada.* I understand that accepting the 2 free books and gifts places me under no obligation to buy anything. I can always return a shipment and cancel at any time. The free books and gifts are mine to keep no matter what I decide.

225/326 HDN GNND

Name (please print)

Address   Apt. #

City   State/Province   Zip/Postal Code

Mail to the **Reader Service:**
IN U.S.A.: P.O. Box 1341, Buffalo, NY 14240-8531
IN CANADA: P.O. Box 603, Fort Erie, Ontario L2A 5X3

Want to try 2 free books from another series? Call 1-800-873-8635 or visit www.ReaderService.com.

*Terms and prices subject to change without notice. Prices do not include sales taxes, which will be charged (if applicable) based on your state or country of residence. Canadian residents will be charged applicable taxes. Offer not valid in Quebec. This offer is limited to one order per household. Books received may not be as shown. Not valid for current subscribers to Harlequin Desire books. All orders subject to approval. Credit or debit balances in a customer's account(s) may be offset by any other outstanding balance owed by or to the customer. Please allow 4 to 6 weeks for delivery. Offer available while quantities last.

Your Privacy—The Reader Service is committed to protecting your privacy. Our Privacy Policy is available online at www.ReaderService.com or upon request from the Reader Service. We make a portion of our mailing list available to reputable third parties that offer products we believe may interest you. If you prefer that we not exchange your name with third parties, or if you wish to clarify or modify your communication preferences, please visit us at www.ReaderService.com/consumerschoice or write to us at Reader Service Preference Service, P.O. Box 9062, Buffalo, NY 14240-9062. Include your complete name and address.

HD20R